ACTIVATE LOVE MODE

PRAISE FOR SPORTSTER THE CAT

Once every so often the world hears a new voice. Judy Howard is the person to whom that voice belongs.

— BEN REEDING

Stunning!

— LONGTIME READER

Judy Howard writes from the heart and hits you in the gut.

— FELLOW AUTHOR

ALSO BY JUDY HOWARD & SPORTSTER

<u>Coast to Coast Series</u>

Coast to Coast with A Cat and A Ghost

Going Home with A Cat and A Ghost

<u>Masada Series</u>

Masada's Marine

Masada's Mission

MORE FROM JUDY HOWARD

Truck Stop

<u>Autobiographical</u>

Grieving Gift

BOOKS GHOST WRITTEN BY SPORTSTER THE CAT

<u>Feline Fury Series</u>

Activate Lion Mode

Activate Love Mode

ACTIVATE

Love Mode

JUDY HOWARD

& Sportster the Cat

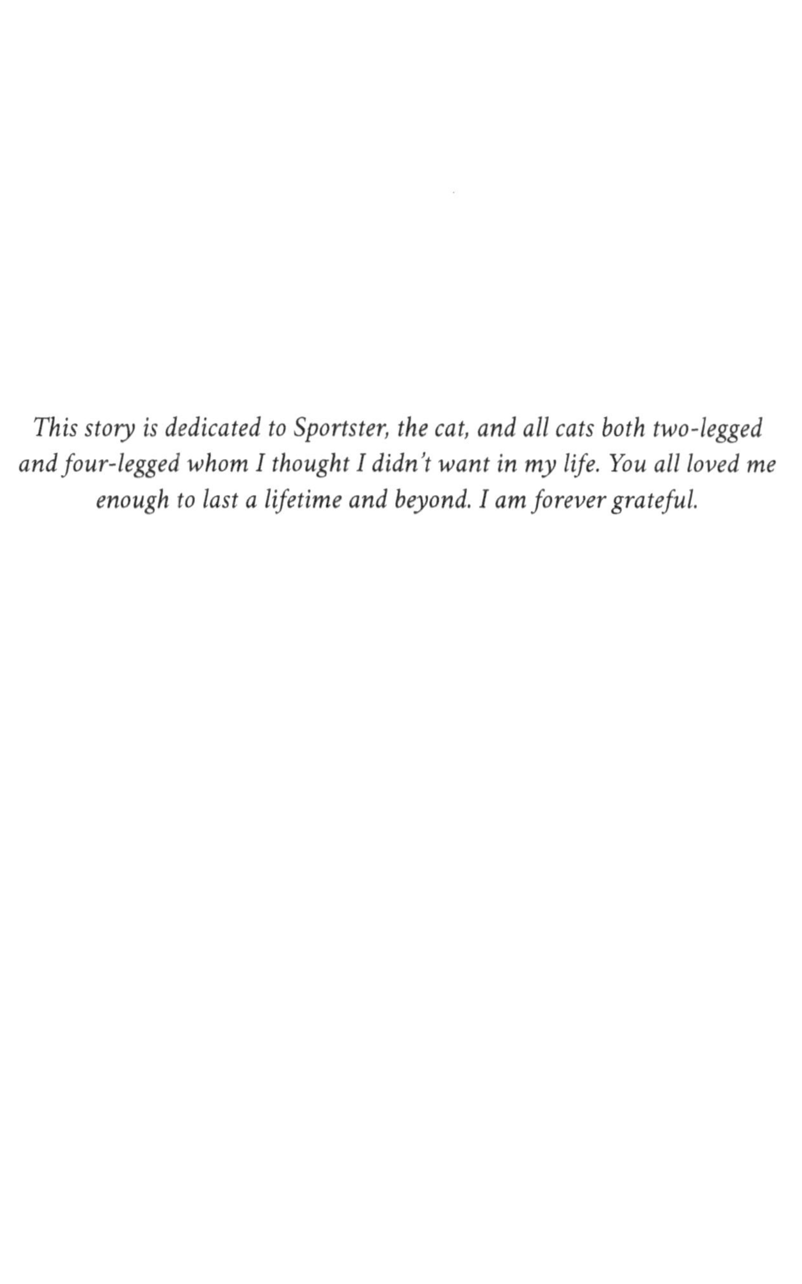

This story is dedicated to Sportster, the cat, and all cats both two-legged and four-legged whom I thought I didn't want in my life. You all loved me enough to last a lifetime and beyond. I am forever grateful.

INTRODUCTION

Sportster is not just an old, coddled cat, he has also served as his mom's muse while she penned her novels and gave writing lectures across the U.S.

When his mom turns off the coastal highway onto the narrow, tree-shrouded river road to their new forested home, Sportster can't shake the apocalyptic sense his next adventure is going to put Alice in Wonderland's trip down the rabbit hole to shame.

Hardly settled in their new home, Sportster's fast-approaching senior years begin to unearth haunting dreams of his lost love, Petunia. When bolder-than-life images of Petunia appear on his mom's computer screen confusion sets in. Or is it dementia? Is she real or a ghost? Has she come for him? Or is she calling for him to come to her?

The lure of his golden-eyed mystic Petunia drives him to revisit his long-ago kitten decisions when he abandoned his family and her. Is it too late to go back, to do the right thing? To make his amends? Should he, could he abandon his loving mom who has provided a charmed life that most cats and even their humans envy?

In everyone's life, there comes a time when we must face the errors of our past. When we are forced to make the hard choices. When we must Activate Love Mode.

Sportster's time has come, but has he waited too long?

CHAPTER ONE

I was a traveling cat. I had seen this entire country through the windshield of a Winnebago motorhome which my author mom calls The Big Story. I had slept in forty-five of the fifty states and had the pleasure of sniffing tree trunks of the Florida palms to the California redwoods. A full food dish and a cozy bed to curl up in next to my mom have always been my dearest possessions.

Unless it was a trip to the vet, Mom rarely took me for a pleasure ride in our Smart Car which she had christened the Short Story. So, when she packed me into my carrier and toted me out to the little car instead of the motorhome, it was not a good sign.

When I peered through the mesh window of my carrier and noticed she had turned away from the beach, away from town, and thankfully away from the veterinarian, I wondered what was up. She had crammed The Short Story full of everything I owned—my catnip toys, food, and bathroom accessories. I may be an old cat, but as she turned down a narrow two-lane road, the promise of another adventure still made my tail twitch.

The tires hummed along the narrow road. Trees surrounded our bubble of a car and murmured, "Hush, hush." Anticipation tickled up my spine with a shiver. I could not help but feel this journey was going to put Alice in Wonderland's adventure down the rabbit hole to shame.

Even The Short Story held its breath with expectancy as we proceeded away from the beach, out of town, and down the shaded, tree-lined route. The tires whispered as they tiptoed along the two-lane asphalt.

We passed homes nearly concealed in thick green vegetation, with only their windows, like watchful wild eyes, reflecting the sun. Each structure was dressed in some shade of the emerald forest surrounding us as if the color was a requirement to exist in this vibrant, renewable world.

The Short Story crept along, reluctant to disturb the congregation of trees that bordered each side of the thoroughfare and threatened to swallow us. Like the robes of worshippers, moss draped from their boughs. The branches reached across the road, creating a tunnel with few possibilities to make amends to the route.

My excitement drained. But Mom, like most humans, puttered along, chattering cluelessly, unaware of the ominous omen.

"Sportster, you're going to be so excited when you see our new place. It's a mansion compared to The Big Story. Windows everywhere! You'll be able to lay in the sun and hear the birds sing and the squirrels chatter as they flit from tree to tree." She reached over, patted my head, and scratched my chin. "And wait 'til you see the deer up close and personal!"

The Sort Story weaved, right, then left, following the moss-covered curves that led us deeper into the shadowy forest. My tummy churned. I thought I might upchuck my Fancy Feast breakfast. Occasional openings in the thick foliage revealed a blue-green ribbon of water. The satin channel, with gentle sparkling ripples, wound and twisted, as if it were escaping the dark woods for the sunbathed seashore that we were leaving behind.

Earlier that morning, during our walk on the beach, thick fog muffled the sound of the ocean's pounding waves. But now, the low clouds floated atop the moody river, alongside us, as if tracking our journey, or were they hiding the river's stealthy escape from the forest?

Mom's foot hit the brakes, and she jerked the wheel. I crouched down into the passenger seat as our little car rocked and rolled. My mind flashed back to the past and… the accident.

It was our motorhome that had begun to rock and roll. It carried us down a road very similar to the one we now traveled. But then it was the Olympic Forest we dared to intrude. And just like then, I worried our little car and my life might be turned upside down. I held my breath and dug my back claws into the seat.

But the accident in the Olympic Forest story is for another time. This day Mom's sharp turn didn't capsize us. She had only taken a right off the river road. The car groaned up, up, and up the unnamed, less traveled back road. Climbing, the tires spun, and the engine whined. Straight up, until I thought we would clear the treetops. But at the peak of the hill, we bumped and bopped, and with one final yank on the wheel and a grinding growl from the tiny car's wheels, Mom made a back-legged turn, rolled into a wide driveway, and came to a stop.

"Okay, Sportster. Here we are! Welcome to our new home!"

I stretched up and peered out the window. Our home and the buildings we had passed, as well as the mossy asphalt roadway leading us here, all appeared out of place. Like the other homes on the river road, our home had also been captured by the trees. Only a corner of the house pushed past the dense growth. I shivered. Our home was white.

Mom turned the key and killed the motor. A stillness washed over us. I sent her a questioning look. The windows of the house gaped at us through the foliage.

Her eyes met mine. "You feel that, too? The Peace? And the Quiet?" She gathered me up, held me in front of her face, and gave me a big, hard kiss on my nose. I scoffed at her enthusiasm and wiggled loose from her embrace.

"Come on. I'll show you around."

I'd have to do a lot of investigating before I called this place home.

CHAPTER TWO

From the safety of the car, I studied our new pad. Like a stag elk making his stand, it stood bravely challenging the encroaching ivy, blackberry bushes, and trees.

I planted my front paws on the edge of the car's half-opened window and scanned the yard. Posed on a stump, a squirrel crouched, twitching his nose. He raised on his haunches, looked me in the eye, and swished his bush of a tail back and forth.

"Hey!" I chirped.

He held his stance, so I chirped again and twitched my tail. He scrambled off the stump, bounded through the ivy and thick ferns, and scampered up a nearby tree. When he reached a comfortable height, he circled the trunk, peeked from behind it, and then waved his tail at me again.

I turned to Mom who shot me a big grin. "Looks like you've made your first friend." She gathered me in her arms again. "Come on. I'll show you our new home." Snapping my leash onto my harness she lifted me out of the car.

If the river road had led us down a rabbit hole, then in contrast, the house and yard opened up a new world alive with a wilderness of aromas that tingled my senses. Mom tugged at my leash, but I was in no hurry. Every rock, every bush, even the dirt, was like a message board, scribbled with strange scents in different languages. I wanted to check out each one.

A bug as fat as it was long scurried across my path. It hid under a rock before I could pounce. Pawing and pulling at the stone, I turned it over. Underneath a curious community of roly-poly bugs came alive as they scurried about to escape my intrusion and the harsh daylight.

Now I was eager to explore. I tugged on my leash and led Mom onward down the path. A set of stairs carried us up to a long, wide deck. I like high places. They offer new perspectives.

To my surprise, our home was not being held captive. Instead, it was as if it had climbed a tree. It perched like a nest in this emerald world and offered a bird's-eye view.

Feeling invisible and unreachable I studied the mossy blanket of a road below and the melancholy river. Several families drifted by in paddle boats and kayaks waving and splashing at one another. Their laughter floated up the hill to where I sat mesmerized. I now scoffed at any foolish and fearful doubts I had imagined about this place and let them disperse in the breeze. My new pad was a penthouse.

A bird, bluer than the bluest sky broke my trance. It blurted out a call, "Jay. Jay."

Mom pointed at the cackling bird. "Look. The Blue Jay's saying good morning!" Mom extended my leash out to its full ten feet and wrapped the handle around a deck chair leg. "You wait here. Talk to your new friend while I unlock the door."

As Mom crossed the deck, the Jay hopped along a branch and cackled again. This time his call was sharp and intimidating. "EEYAAWK!"

Was he calling me out? Trying to scare me? Birds don't like cats. I supposed he didn't like me invading his neighborhood. I tugged on my leash, trying to put distance between me and the angry bird.

"EEYAAWK!" This time his shrill call pierced my ears. My fur stood on end. We were probably close to his nest. I'd dealt with angry birds before. If I didn't heed the Jay's warning, his next move would be a nosedive, pecking and clawing me until I retreated. But his focus was not on me. His beak pointed to the airspace above. I followed his line of sight.

A raptor flew lazy, ominous circles overhead. My fur spiked, and I arched my back. The Jay was warning me! He bellowed out one last cry and took cover in thicker vegetation.

Once in Montana, I witnessed the power of an eagle's lethal talons when he took out a young raccoon for dinner… and not to a restaurant. I remember hoping I would never suffer the same fate.

"EEEYYAAAWK!" This was not the Jay's simulation. The shrill call was not the Jay's. It was the raptor calling me out. It was not a warning, but a death call that shot through me like a thousand needles. The big bird belted out one more screech, hung in the sky for a moment, and then, in a nosedive, barreled downward like a bullet aimed at its target. His target? Me!

I arched my back, spiked my fur, and I screamed out my death wish that I hoped would shake his feathers off. Alarmed by the screeching and my cries, Mom rushed to me.

The huge bird's wings cast a dark shadow over the width of the deck. A swoosh of air from his powerful wings slapped my face. I cringed. I smelled the dried blood on his razor-sharp talons, now only inches from my face. I reared up. My blood-curdling scream exploded in my ears. The image of that Montana Eagle flashed before my eyes. The coon's bloody entrails dripped from his beak. I dove behind Mom and flattened my body against the deck.

Like an enraged mother cat, Mom shrieked out her death sentence, "NO!" Her foot shot out at the precise moment the bird braked to grab his dinner. Me! Her small foot landed solidly against my attacker's breast.

The raptor thrashed his wings, trying to regain balance. His claws raked and scraped the wooden deck as he tried to change tack. His wings pounded the surrounding air. His struggling claws grated and scratched across the entire deck like a freight train coming into the station, but his deadly talons had missed their mark.

In a lifetime of seconds, he achieved lift. With each beat of his massive wings against the blue sky, he shrank, smaller and smaller, until he became only a dot.

I gasped for air and lunged for the edge of the deck just as Mom swooped me up. Pressing me close to her chest, her arms trembled. Or was it me trembling? Petting me, she cooed, "It's okay! It's okay. Poor baby! I won't let anyone get you." She held me so tight it was hard to breathe. I buried my face in the crook of her arm while she kissed me, hugged me, and carried me into our new home.

CHAPTER THREE

Once in the house, Mom's heartbeat still raced. "Everything's okay now. You're okay. That was so scary. You poor thing. Everything's okay now. Mommy will never let any big bad bird hurt you." Her cheery voice squeaked an octave higher. "Let's check out our new house, okay?"

With shaky hands, she set me down. Her fingers jerked as she fumbled with the snap and unhooked my leash. "You go explore. It'll take your mind off that mean bird."

An expansive room with golden wood flooring lay out before me. The place smelled of fresh paint. French doors and floor-to-ceiling windows promised a safe view of the outdoors from everywhere in the room. Warily, I made my way across the room and peered through the lower pane of those doors, only to jump straight up in the air. Hair on end and side-stepping, I backed away.

A cat stared at me through the glass.

With my back arched, ears laid back, growling, and spitting, I faced it off. Ignoring my challenge, it did not move. Was it only my reflection? I lifted my chin, shrugged, and started to walk away.

But I stopped in my tracks, hearing a meow so soft I thought it might be the wind whispering in the trees. Half-turning, I examined the image more closely. Green eyes embedded in black, tiger-striped fur stared at me. A seductive twitch of its tail told me it was not a reflection, and *it* was a she. Not my imagination. Not my reflection.

Encouraged, she had my attention she mewed again, just a bit louder.

I returned her comment with a hiss, a spit, and a low growl. I didn't want her to get any ideas about coming inside.

Undaunted, her jungle green eyes answered with an erotic slow blink. She gazed steadily at me. She must not have heard me. I hissed, spit, and growled again, this time louder and longer.

And still, she did not get my message.

She raised her soft paw, ever so slowly and gently. Reaching toward me with a feathery touch she pressed it against the glass that separated us. She mewed, again.

I grunted. I've met plenty of pretty ones who fancied me during my motorhome travels in the past, but I have always been a traveling cat. After a day, a week, or a month, I always moved on. I may not be traveling anymore but now I'm old. Too old for a fling. I stretched. Flexing my toes and twitching my tail I turned my back to her and resumed my investigation of my new digs that Mom was calling home.

A wood-burning stove squatted between two floor-to-ceiling windows.

Golden puddles of sunshine warmed the knotty pine floor at the base of each. I peered out.

The view knocked my little white socks off.

It was as if I had climbed a tree and announced to the world, "I am king!" I dreamed of climbing trees, but without front claws, the skill escaped me. But look at me now! The view extended over the treetops and went on forever. Maybe this place wasn't so bad. I could become the top cat. No wonder the little missy on the patio was enamored. I plunked myself down in the sunshine and preened. Spitting on my paws, I wiped my face, and ears, and touched up my tail, and then I let out a satisfied chirp.

My survey led me into a room adjoining the kitchen with walls of glass. Potted plants adorned shelves that seemed to float. Plants inside. I liked drinking plant water from their saucers.

In the small spaces of our motorhome, I could spring from the back of our couch in the living room across a narrow aisle and land on the kitchen counter. But here there was no easy way to jump onto the kitchen counter except from the floor. I hoped his old man could still make a jump that high.

I moseyed on down the hall sniffing familiar scents, Mom's, mine, and those of strangers. A small room on the left, a bathroom, and then at the end of the hall a bedroom with a small window.

Outside, a narrow mossy trail led up an embankment to a waterfall that trickled lazily over river stones, splashing its way into a pond below. As much as the sleepy pond scene made me want to nap beside it, the secrecy of the area at the end of the path with trees shrouding its entrance equally intrigued me. Even though shadows floated across the opening left by the parting branches and even though a shiver crawled up my spine, I wanted to explore its mystical allure.

With a stiff gait, I headed back to the main room. The green-eyed cat remained on the other side of the French doors where I had left her. She squeaked out another mew of invitation and again I hissed as I padded by.

Yet still, she squeaked out another meow as I hurried by.

I found Mom chattering on her cell in the sunny plant room, but she raised a brow when she heard me spit at the cat.

"When the realtor showed the house, she was pregnant. I figured she belonged to the sellers. But then when I finally moved in, I found a note they'd left explaining, even though Girl—original name, right? Even though she was wild, they'd been feeding her, and they asked me to please continue."

I growled under my breath. I hope her kittens aren't hanging around, too.

"I think she's already had her kittens. She's lost weight and looks pretty fine. But Sportster is hissing at her every time he sees her."

While Mom talked, she moved into the kitchen. She placed the coffee carafe under the faucet and began filling it. Running water! I'd worked up a thirst. I studied the countertop's height, crouched, and leaped. Perfect landing. Yes! Who says I'm too old?

Mom talked on. "But she just ignored his rejection. Didn't even blink." Mom chuckled.

I didn't think it was funny.

"I swear she gave him the peace sign. She reached out her paw and touched the glass pane." Mom laughed even louder.

I sat at the sink's edge and glared at her. She shut off the water and poured the carafe of water into the coffeepot. To get her attention, I meowed.

"Oh, gotta go. His Highness is calling for a drink from the faucet. Looks like he's making himself at home. Talk to you later." Still giggling, she lay the cell phone on the counter. Now focused on me, she turned the water back on to a thin stream. A couple of licks proved it clear and cold. As I lapped, my irritation melted. Finishing, I checked out the view. More windows lined the length of the counter and the morning sun poured in. Another bird's-eye view and a warm nesting place for me.

Back to unpacking Mom rooted through boxes stacked on the sunroom table. "There's so much yet to do. Later I'll try to take you for a walk outside and you can explore."

Go back outside? I don't think so! A nap in the sunshine is what I needed for my old bones. Laying down, I rested my chin on my paws and watched the squirrel scurrying about in the front yard. His tail flicked and flagged as he stopped and started every few steps he took. High on another branch, I spotted the Jay who had warned me of the raptor's attack. I will never forget his kindness. I thought about Wild Girl and wondered what her story was. The leaves of the treetops whispered a wind-song lullaby. Its notes drifted through an open window somewhere in the house, lulling me to sleep. Memories clung to the lighthearted notes which lifted me and carried me like a leaf floating down a lazy river and into the past.

CHAPTER FOUR

The memories of Mom's nose nudging my siblings and me, fussing over us before she left for a night of hunting gave me a tickling, funny feeling. Every night she chirped and purred and praised us while she licked and cleaned our faces. But then just before she disappeared into the darkness, she scolded us. "Never leave the den. Ever! While I hunt, you stay here where you're safe."

The worry in her voice prompted me to ask about my dad. He had not been home for what seemed like a long time in my kitten world. And when I asked Mom never tired of telling me his story. And big eyed I never tired of hearing it.

Nudging me close, her eyes clouded as she dug up her memories. She purred and gazed into the starry night sky. "His eyes flash like jewels against his black fur."

"A wild spirit he is, your father. He's no kitten. Some call him Ice. Those who love him know him as fun-loving and always ready to help out a hungry stray in need." Her eyes darkened as she continued her story. "Under that coat of kindness is an icy coolness if another cat disrespects him or anyone he loves. You don't want to uncover that layer. That's why those who foolishly crossed him call him Ice. But Grandpa and the rest of the family call him Hook because of the crook in his tail. Remember the hook?"

With her paw, she pushed and pulled at me, making sure I was tucked close to my brothers and sister. "Some call your dad Outlaw. Others claim he may be possessed by the devil…" At this point in the story, her eyes drifted to some faraway place, and she sighed dreamily. Her purring took on a deep, guttural tone. "I don't care what others think. I've talked to the teary-eyed mothers whose kittens he rescued from the Army. They all worshipped him knowing he'd saved their loved ones from the horrors of the Army." She hung her head and sighed. "I know he isn't always here for us, but I can't deny him his passion for helping the unfortunate. It's his calling. When I look into his eyes, I see the stars and the moon, and I feel like I'm flying."

At this part of the story, Mom would pace around the den checking that all was secure, and then fussing needlessly once again over each of us to make sure we were snugged in. And then changing her gait, she returned to Dad's story.

"Every street cat knows about the People's Humane Army. The Army is our most frightening predator. The stories of their so-called humane activities have been passed down to you by your great-grandpa, to your grandpa, and now to your dad. The People's Humane Army believes there are too many of us. If they catch you, most times you're never seen again. They stick needles in you."

Mom's eyes glassed over, and her tail switched back and forth like a whip. "The lucky ones who escape wear *the Mark*, a nick in their ear to prove, if caught again, they are not a first offender." She took a deep breath and shook her head as if returning from somewhere far away. "So. when your Uncle Tux went missing, your father, believing he'd been kidnapped by the People's Humane Army, joined the resistance."

She flattened her ears and muttered something. Her words tumbled out as a growl, and she switched her tail back and forth. "That's our father and grandpa. They support the resistance.

Always watching out for the lost and alone, and the others who prefer to live free. So, when Uncle Tux went missing your dad joined up."

Mom sat at the den's entrance again, gazing into the darkness. "I was lucky he stayed as long as he did. I never kidded myself. I knew one day he would give in to his calling."

She turned to me and purred. "Your eyes glow with the same light." A cloud of sadness enfolded her. Her tail swayed slowly back and forth with the heaviness of a rain-soaked branch in the breeze. "When he couldn't stand the injustice anymore, he made that hard decision he had been wrestling with, probably since he was your age." Her ears flattened and her eyes darkened. "He let loose a long, festering caterwaul, and I knew he was going to go. And then, with a swish of that crooked tail, he leaped back over the fence separating us from the busy world..." She hung her head. Her shoulders slumped. She, too, let go a long, tired sigh. "He was gone."

When Dad left, the responsibility of me and my five siblings fell on Mom. Mom may have seen him as a hero, but my stomach knotted up when I thought about the hardships she suffered—hunting all night, every night, because of his absence. I was young but old enough to see how she struggled to feed her family. She grew bone thin.

Worrying over my sibling's hungry mews kept me awake. Their desperate cries killed my appetite. One morning, Mom returned home, her tail dragging on the ground and her ears flattened in defeat. She didn't even look up as she entered. I was only a kitten, but I read the hollow despair in her eyes. I couldn't bear it any longer. I had to do something. I refused the meager share she offered me. After she collapsed in exhausted sleep, I struck out on my own. I would be one less mouth for her to feed. I would learn to hunt and take Dad's place. I'd show Mom she didn't need him.

Handicapped by my youth, my hunting lacked the patience and skill that comes with experience. After a few days, my valiant thoughts of helping Mom and feeding my siblings waned. The weeks passed with scant success. Without the cunning and patience of experience, I pounced at birds and rabbits only for them to easily escape my clumsy efforts. I resorted to eating bugs. My life became cold nights and hunger pangs. Every night I wrestled with the temptation of returning home to Mom's loving warmth.

My shivers, but not from the cold. made for restless nights. I lay awake listening to the all too frequent gut-wrenching cries of death from the weak creatures who had lost their battle with fate. I trembled knowing every night that passed brought my turn closer.

One morning just when the world was at its darkest, a warm sun peeked through the bushes where I hid. I took it as a sign from the heavens. A whimper of hope reminded me of Mom's warmth and the way she curled herself around me. I wanted to fall asleep wrapped up in her purring fur. Just for one night.

I abandoned my valiant convictions to save Mom and my family.

The beauty of the day bolstered my will to go home. I didn't know the way, but instinct steered me. I had wandered past the greenery of the countryside and had to sneak along the city's sidewalks. Slinking down the concrete paths I simmered with anger for Dad whom I blamed for my devastating humiliation and feelings of failure.

Dusk had encroached on the sunny afternoon as I found myself out of noisy city limits and back in the deceiving quiet of the country. I crept through the overgrown grass toward the abandoned bunkhouse with its peeling paint at the edge of the city. I slipped under the porch and into the den's warm dry space… warm, dry… and empty.

I sniffed every nook and corner, and under the dry leafy bed Petunia where had lain, trying to catch Mom's scent. Only a stale whiff remained. The ground, once warmed by my siblings, was bare and cold on my feet. My heart sank. My family was gone. In their place, a foreboding fear wrapped around me like a heavy coat, making it difficult to stand. My shaky legs felt like logs.

With an anxious heart, I rooted and pawed under every stick and stone for a stray morsel of food. Not a crumb remained. This was not home anymore. I crawled outside and collapsed on the porch. As I rested my chin on my cold paws, my eyes caught a movement. Snagged on a branch, a hunk of hair fluttered in the last light of day. Mom's faint scent drifted to me. My heart skipped. Jumping up, I trotted toward it just as the wind loosened it. It whirled into the air. I swatted at it but missed. Too weak to even whine, I watched the breeze carry away the last evidence of my family.

CHAPTER FIVE

The gate at the end of the driveway leading from the bunkhouse opened up to the bustle of the city. Speeding traffic, banging trash cans, and annoying car horns honked like a flock of geese. But the city redeemed itself by offering up an array of smells... the most enticing, the aroma of food.

During those dark days, I hid under cars, in bushes, and behind trash bins, living off discarded food wrappers and an occasional ice cream cone I plodded through the days growing weaker and more distraught. I wondered, what's the use? The hate for my father's abandonment festered and grew like an angry boil, and yet it spurred me on.

One particular morning, the sun came up, heating the earth under my paws and giving my waning spirit an extra charge. A wrinkled food wrapper carried by the sultry breeze drifted by. Its tantalizing cheesy aroma awakened the needs of my shrunken tummy. I set out on the chase.

The promising morsel floated only a whisker's length away. I crouched, rocked back and forth, preparing to attack. Just before I pounced, the wind snatched it up. I leaped skyward. Stretching, reaching, I clawed it from the air.

Pride for my successful catch combined with the anticipation of a good meal, no matter how meager, fired up my spirits. As my feet landed on the ground and before I could catch my breath, I stumbled backward choking on a rancid odor.

A smelly gray dog stood so close his hypnotizing, blood-red eyes froze me with fear. The greasy hair on his back stood on end like the needles of a bristle-cone pine tree. His tail extended behind him, a tattered flag. He snarled, breaking my trance.

Shivers raked up my spine like toenails clawing a tin trash can and I gasped, then gagged as I inhaled his rank, sour breath. Blinking, I tried to clear my watery, burning eyes. The disputed cheesy wrapper fluttered above us, and then, like a tease, it floated down and came to rest in the narrow space between mine and the dog's noses. It quivered against the light breeze provoking us.

The canine bared his rotting teeth and snapped at my face. Choking again, I hung my head and slumped away as the thrill of my catch drained from me, along with any hope of even a meager meal.

As I turned to retreat, the dinner still unclaimed, surrendered not to the gnarly dog but to nature as it once again danced away on the wind. The angry canine's red eyes flashed, and he snarled as if his loss were my fault.

Eyeing the safety under a trash bin, I turned my tail to skedaddle just as a bolt of yellow fur shot past me.

A tabby ball of fur with claws extended flung itself upon the dog's bristled back. The burly gray, whose shadow moments before had boldly darkened my path, now wailed in pain. His toenails scraped the asphalt as he dug for traction to make his escape.

But his blonde attacker screamed out her own challenge while she clung on like a veteran bull rider at a rodeo. She rode him the full eight seconds halfway down the block. And then, as if claiming her victory, jumped off, allowing the gnarly canine to disappear around the corner.

The boss bombshell skidded to a stop. Assured her prey was indeed not coming back, she sat down as if to catch her breath; I assumed. Then, with a satisfied switch of her tail, she preened. She finished with a confident chirp and another jerk from her fluffy tail. Snatching up the cheese wrapper, she raised her nose skyward, and with the lightness of confidence, she trotted back to me.

The wrapper flapped against her soft round face, as she padded up to me and sat down primly in front of me. I could have reached over and grabbed the disputed morsel she now claimed as hers, but I didn't want another confrontation. I dropped my tail low, hung my head, and once again turned to leave. No dinner tonight.

But when she dropped the dinner at my feet, I paused. She extended her once menacing paw, now unthreatening and soft, and pinned the tasty prize so it wouldn't blow away. Then she waited.

Her big round eyes stared into mine while her golden tail undulated back and forth in a way even a young cat could recognize. Purring, she bent down, pushed the wrapper toward me, and chirped.

Unsure, I remained glued in place. Could she be serious? Was this a trick? The dinner's aroma of cheese and fish wafted across the space between us. I sniffed. My stomach growled loud enough for her to hear. I hoped she knew it was not me making a stand, but only my stomach. I looked away as a drool of saliva landed on my paw.

She chirped another mew, one of reassurance. I squeaked out a questioning tweet in return.

She meowed once more, this time with sharp impatience. Before she could change her mind, I pounced. Ripping at the morsels on the wax wrapper, I devoured the cheesy chunks of fish, wax paper, and all. No meal has ever tasted so good. When finished, I looked up, flushed at my lack of control, and pretended to clean my face.

"I'm Petunia. My friends call me Tune 'cause I like tuna and..." She sent me another seductive message with a long blink and a loud purr. "...Because of my name." Her deep golden eyes zeroed in on my hesitating gaze. She twitched her tail and once again gave me a long slow blink that made my tummy do flip-flops and not because of the meal I'd just eaten.

She turned away and proceeded to saunter down the street. My heart sank as I sat watching, hips swaying one way, her tail swinging the other way.

Glancing over her shoulder, she called out to me. "Follow me."

I snapped out of my trance and galloped after her. Drawing alongside her, I stole a glance in her direction. Her nose was the pinkest, and except for a black smudge on her cheek, maybe an oil stain, she was a picture of perfection, worth a Lion King's ransom.

Without even a glance in my direction, she began to speak. "Dogs are the easiest to bluff. With the right attitude, you can hiss and growl at a German shepherd ten times your size and send him running. And when you pull it off, they're terrified, thinking you are crazed and rabid and out of control."

Swinging around, she landed nose to nose in front of me, hissing and growling. More than startled, I jumped back. Hair on end, I tripped over my feet. As I untangled my legs. "Tune" laughed and stepped away. Lowering her tail, she swished it slowly. "And that's the way it's done." She purred with amusement.

I was young. She made me feel safe and loved. What would have become of me if she had not come to my rescue that day? Lost, hungry, and abandoned, she was my hero.

I trailed behind her with hope in my heart as she led me across the expanse of a yard and past two flowering mimosas trees flanking a run-down bunkhouse not far from the house where I was born. My step faltered as I pushed back the memories.

Untended evergreens surrounded a weather-worn porch held together by a rusty railing and peeling yellow paint. It had a sadness about it, reminding me of my losses. She led me through the thick wall of evergreens and into her den.

*　*　*　*

During the following weeks, with Petunia's encouragement and guidance, my confidence grew. I soon learned to outwit any gnarly cat who wanted to poach our territory. As my fierce side developed and I sent the last of our last competitors high-tailing down the street, Petunia butted her head against mine, purred loudly, and kissed my nose. "Congratulations. You're now a graduate warrior of Petunia's School of Street Smarts."

My chest swelled with pride and confidence. My legs turned squishy like the worms I played with after a rain. And once again, my tummy flip-flopped. I returned her affections, kissing the furry smudge on her cheek that I once considered an imperfection. Now, I adored it and the surprising but pleasant effect she stirred in me.

My whole world had shifted. I strutted. I was the Lion King. Nothing scared me. Although Petunia proved herself as a scrapper, she kept her appearance up. One would think she just stepped out of a Beverly Hills pet salon. And yet she didn't hesitate to fight for what she believed in. And she could fight a good fight. I found a few scarred badges from her battles when I groomed her…

With Petunia's guidance, I came of age. We hunted together; we ate together, and we slept together. We watched each other's back on our nightly prowls. After our shared meals, I groomed her tirelessly until her coat puffed like a soft cloud. When she slept, warm and satisfied, only then would I snuggle up to her sweetness and sleep. I was King.

CHAPTER SIX

A gentle rain soaked the ground overnight and the gray sky melted into red and gold as the sun fired up on the horizon. Across the street, a trash can crashed to the pavement, shattering the silence, like the starting gun at a racetrack. It was trash day and the challenge to survive began.

A coyote, the cause of the loud clatter, scrounged through the spilled garbage, strewing the contents across the asphalt as if it were a buffet table. He ate in a frenzy until he spotted the big-bellied greasy cat ambling up to his buffet.

Like Wiley Coyote in the Road Runner cartoons, the wild dog paused, assessing the feline's attitude. Nothing was said between the two. The message in the narrowed cat eyes spoke volumes. Wiley lowered his head and tucked his tail. Surrendering his find, he slinked away. The greasy feline studied every movement as the dog trotted down the shiny street that was still wet from the night's rain.

I scrutinized the wild cat from where I crouched in the evergreens by my den's door. Matted with dirt and oil, the cat's heavy black fur blended with the dirty asphalt, making him appear as a shadow moving across the ground. Only his tail was untouched by his crude lifestyle. Feathery and light, it jerked back and forth, listing in the breeze as he stared at the dog's retreat.

Trash day on the streets played out the same every week. The greaser floated onto the scene, catching his many canine marks off guard. Spitting and hissing, he faced off with each stray dog. His toenails scraped across the ground as his big-eyed victims scratched for traction in a desperate attempt to escape his razor claws. Tufts of fur flew into the air, setting off the blackbirds who cawed like a razed crowd at a cockfight. There would be no guests at the Greaser's table.

When the coyote gained a comfortable distance from the feast, only then did the Greaser grunt in victory. He gave his airy tail a swift switch, and then, like the help after a wedding party, he began picking through the scant remains.

Hunkered down in my evergreen shelter, I remained dry but shivered. Mesmerizing raindrops slid off the evergreen fronds and tap-tapped into silvery puddles on the saturated ground. My tummy growled so loud I feared the black Rottweiler who lived in the yellow house on the corner might hear.

❋ ❋ ❋ ❋ ❋ ❋

When the Greaser had eaten his fill, he licked his paws, washed his face, and ambled down to the corner as if he owned the world. I thought it bold of him that he did not increase his pace but instead sauntered past the Rottweiler's yellow house even though the garage door was open.

Last week Petunia and I traveled the same route past the Rott's house on our way home after a good night of hunting. Light-footed and lighthearted, we ignored Petunia's rule to detour the Rott's house if the garage door stood open. Had she forgotten? Or had I distracted her?

Petunia and I paused on our stroll home from hunting to laugh at a squirrel scampering up a tree. Seconds later, that bad-ass black Rott charged from the depths of the open garage. The broad-muscled dog was fast for his size. He reached Petunia first. Caught off guard, she yowled as his boxy jaws clamped down on her. Spittle and fur flew as he shook her. I stood by in terror.

I could hardly believe what I saw. My heroine put her hurt on her attacker. She dug her claws into an eyeball. Now he yowled. His eye dripped blood. The dog reversed tack. Shaking his head violently, he tried to fling her off; she stuck like Velcro.

He howled even louder. This time for mercy. Free of his jaws, Petunia shimmied off his square nose. While she made her descent, her claws raked down the Rott's neck and chest. Rivers of blood, hers or the Rott's I couldn't tell, flowed after her. Hair on end, she found her footing on solid ground. Ready to fight the Rott to the death, she screamed out a high-pitched death call.

But to no avail. He had already turned tail and ran. Howling all the way, he vanished into the dark depths of his garage.

That was a week ago. Now I glanced over my shoulder and into the den. Petunia still lay on her side upon a bed of pine needles, her wounds raw and oozing. I padded to her and kissed the furry black smudge on her cheek. She whimpered in a restless sleep.

I imagined the horrific battle scars Petunia would bear—if she lived. They would always remind me of my inability to protect her. I hung my head. Then, with a sharp switch of my tail, I shoved the guilt aside. Regret has no place in a cat's life. You do the best you can and bury it.

CHAPTER SEVEN

Again, it was trash day which brought the possibility of a meal no matter how meager presented itself. Yet, I held back. I didn't want to risk confronting anyone let alone the greaser even though my stomach knotted painfully in hunger.

The stray cat's crude bravery and decisive brutality made me think of my dad. I'd bet he was a greaser. A shot of envy and pride penetrated the crust of hate I'd built.

After taking his time and eating his fill, the stray swatted at an empty dog food can he had licked clean and disappeared around the corner. Only then did I creep out from my hidey-hole. I sniffed through the leftover pickings—a piece of toast and an empty tuna can. Not a fancy feast but better than the bugs and a couple of mice that I had survived on last few days. I licked the tuna can clean and carried the crust back to my Petunia.

Weeks uncurled into a month as I faithfully licked and nursed Petunia's wounds. Slowly, she began to recover. For the first time since her injury, but only after my nudging and encouragement did, she joined me hunting. With her by my side, my mood lightened. I bounded ahead on our well-worn hunting path, waited for her to catch up, and then pounced in front of her, dancing and running circles around her. She purred in appreciation but didn't play.

She stopped frequently to rest. Eventually surrendering to her exhaustion, she headed back to the den. I stayed out a little longer hoping to bring something home for dinner. When I did head home.

I walked a little lighter through the petunias that flourished in the untended lawn happy she had joined me even if it was only for a while. I didn't look up. The scent trail of a rabbit drifted past my nose. I spied him further up the path nosing through the patch of flowering petunias searching for clover and dandelions. He hopped along, stopping occasionally, as he rooted in the dead grass. Rain droplets tickled my ears and landed on my nose and whiskers. Annoyed, I shook my head. It would be dark soon so I abandoned the hunt for another day when Petunia could join me.

I ducked into the evergreens encircling the porch as the blackbird in the Mimosa tree cawed his angry warnings. It was always angry, always worried. I hated him and the others liked him. He was the ringleader. Every night he called the others in. They gathered in mass, like thick pepper in the two mimosa trees. They weighed down the limbs until they sagged. And then they quarreled like the talking heads on the news channel Mom watched the squawking and pecking at one another non-stop until darkness set in. Then as if a switch had been flipped, they became deathly quiet.

Crawling through the thick shrubbery into our den I scanned the interior for Petunia. Usually, I found her curled up in our bed of pine needles which had been softened by a blanket of our shredded fur. Outside, the damned birds' raucous chatter raked up my spine. I stopped short then with my eyes swept the den again. No Petunia.

She probably had gone back out looking for me. I thought about going out to find her, but instead, I lay down, curled into a ball, and tucked my nose into my warm belly fur just as the birds called it a day too, and the eerie quiet set in.

Sunlight entered through the small entrance and woke me. I didn't have to open my eyes to know I was alone. Unease crept under my skin. Maybe she was sunning on the porch. I mewed, thumped my tail, and peered out into the yard. The rain had stopped, and the sun hung high in the sky. Still no Petunia.

"Stay clear of the people! Hide! You never know if they are part of the People's Humane Army!" Petunia's instructions rang in my ears. A shiver crept up my spine. Had she not heeded her warnings? Two days passed as I waited for her return. Had she found another? Had she tired of my innocence? Finally, hunger, loneliness, and doubt spurred me on from the safety of the den.

I ventured outside. Wandering the area, my footfall heavy with worry, I tried to catch her trail. Only a couple of months before I had searched for my family.

An aching dread and deep hurt weighed me down. I trudged along our usual paths, now muddy from the rain. First my dad, then my family, and now Petunia. A growl escaped from deep inside. I leaped up onto a cold concrete park bench for a better view of the surroundings. Wet and shivering, I focused on cleaning my muddy paws. The steady licking comforted me.

I didn't see the man who swept me up until it was too late. Petunia's voice screamed inside my head. "Run! Hide!"

I thought my chest might explode from the fear. It pounded so hard I swayed with dizziness. I hissed. I growled. I showed my fangs. My claws met empty air. The man's arms wrapped around me so tight, I couldn't even squirm. His musky scent gagged me. At last, I sank my nails in his arm and held on tight, burying my face in the folds of his arm.

But he plucked me off like a cocklebur and stuffed me into a bag. What was happening? I fought against the darkness yowling and hissing until I ran out of breath. I didn't give up, but feeling faint, I went limp. The bag began to swing. I upchucked.

After a series of rocking and swaying my paws felt solid footing again, and I breathed in a leathery odor. A car engine came to life, its motor vibrated, making the ground shake. We were moving. But where? How was I going to find my way back to the den? Was he a part of the People's Humane Army? I cried out at the thought. What kind of world was this? I couldn't stop trembling. My dad had left and never come back, then my family disappeared, and then Petunia. What had become of them? It looked like I was next. What was going to become of me?

At least I was safe in the darkness of the bag.

CHAPTER EIGHT

My security was short-lived. The car came to a stop. The ground ceased vibrating, and the bag swayed and swung again. My stomach lurched again. A dribble of bile dampened my paws. The outside air changed to an inside-stuffy-animal smell. The People's Humane Army?

I figured I was in the bowels of the building of the People's Humane Army. One hundred dogs erupted in a cacophony of barks, each sounding like that Bad Rottweiler on the corner. Any hope of freedom I had clung to sank into the pit of my stomach.

Then the man began fussing with my bag. Daylight invaded my space. My heart lurched with the possibility of escape. Yet, I held back, too frightened to take the chance against the barking dogs. The man's big hand crawled into the bag, curled around me, and lifted me out. Again, my claws met only air as I twisted and turned in the bright light.

A woman exited the room of the barking dogs. She approached the man who was now focused on trying to calm me down. Her step was light, and her eyes lit up at the sight of me. Grinning, she leaned her face close to mine and wrinkled her nose. She smelled like lilacs.

"Hi!" Her eyes met mine. "What do we have here? Have you come to my grooming salon for a bath?" Her index finger wiped away a tear that had shamelessly escaped my eye. Scratching my chin, then my ears, she peered up and gave the man a questioning look.

He shook his head. "I'm not here to get him groomed. I found this little guy on the street." He patted my head. "I was hoping you could give me directions to the shelter. I figure something's happened to his mother. He's so young and skinny. He doesn't have a collar. I'm afraid he's going to get hit by a car." With his words, the man caught his breath. "I saw your grooming shop and thought you would know where the shelter was." He sounded worried, but the mention of the shelter didn't fool me. He meant the People's Humane Army. Any warm fuzzy feelings I might have had for him died.

The woman turned her attention back to me and rubbed her nose against mine. "You don't need to take him there. We can find a good home for him."

The man's tension drained. His shoulders relaxed. His tight grip on me slackened and his voice lit up. "Really? Great! Because I can't keep him. I have dogs."

Focused on me, she lifted me gently from the man's clutches. Kissing me the top of my head she cuddled me to her breast.

I let out a hopeful mew.

Smiling reassuringly, she reached out to the man, and they shook hands. "Don't worry we'll find this little guy a good home." She rubbed her nose against mine again. "It won't be a problem. He's so cute!" Her breath smelled sweet and clean. With a surge of hope, I butted my head against her chin. I wished the man had brought Petunia too.

The good home ended up being the woman's home. She adopted me.

My "good home" meant action-filled days at the pet grooming salon, chasing tufts of dog hair that floated down from the grooming tables, and teasing the dogs who wanted to play but didn't know how to play cat games.

At day's end, when the world quieted, and the moon shone bright, I cuddled with my new mom. Feeling safe and warm, I started calling her mom even though not a night went by when thoughts of my family and Petunia didn't haunt me. And as sure as a cat pounces on its prey, each time I called her mom, I flinched as a stab of guilt followed, reminding me of the betrayal to my cat mom's memory.

Had the Humane Army captured them? Had their fate been the needle? I worried. How much time did I have with my new mom before she, too, vanished? When sleep did come, nightmarish scenarios about what happened to my family and Petunia played in my mind.

Life has a miraculous way of moving on. Time passed, and I became accustomed to the security and comfort my new home offered. I never scrounged for food again. My new mom didn't see me as a throwaway cat.

We began traveling. We cruised in Mom's motorhome from campground to campground, town to town, and state to state, never loitering for any length of time at our brick-and-mortar home in Southern California. My kitten days were pushed aside and replaced with a series of exciting adventures, exploring new places, meeting new people, and teasing new campground dogs. If we stayed too long in one place, my paws began to itch, and my tail twitched. Like a caged lion, I would pace in anticipation of the adventures waiting on the road ahead.

Memories of my daring exploits with Petunia during our cat-chasing dog experiences still sneak up on me from time to time. Between our exploits of conquering neighborhoods, we romped and played. I may be an old tomcat, but the butterflies still tickle my tummy when I dream of my adventures with my Petunia.

For years, I batted around the idea of going back to the streets in search of her and my family. But the dangers of the journey made my paws sweat and my tummy burn as if an angry bird had ripped it open. So, I shoved away the shadowy memories and sent them scattering into the corners of my mind. They never disappeared. They waited for an opportune moment to pounce back.

CHAPTER NINE

My mind whooshed through the years and back to the present as I blinked awake. While I slept, the puddle of sunshine on the kitchen countertop had moved to the floor in front of the long windows. Now it lay like a golden embossed invitation. I stood and then stretched. Accepting its sunny hospitality, I jumped off the counter, padded to it, and planted myself on the warm floorboards.

Grooming one paw, then the next. I preened. Ten years have passed. These days I enjoy a simple life and simple needs--to be warm in the winter, cool in the summer, and never see the shiny bottom of my food bowl. Oftentimes the day's exertions tire me. In this home in the trees, Mom had settled into a routine, and I had stopped waiting to return to our motorhome.

Wild Girl, who seemed to come with the house, also had a routine. At daybreak, she appeared outside by the French doors. Wherever she spent the night was a mystery to me. There she sang a minstrel's song, encouraging Mom to fill her dish. After eating her fill, she left some kibble for later. It gave me comfort knowing she was getting enough to eat. I wondered if she had ever had a real bath like Mom gave me. And where was her litter box? How did she end up in the wild? I continued to give her the cold shoulder.

Late in the mornings, she patrolled the house's perimeter, then disappeared into the thick cover of Blackberry bushes. A small grove of fruit trees at the bottom of the hill grew apart from the hemlock, pine, and fir trees that took their stand by the creek. Long, leafy ferns and thick moss thrived in their shade and provided endless hidey-holes for the hunted and the hunters, like Wild Girl.

Every afternoon, as regular as the setting sun, Wild Girl showed up on the patio by the French doors. Like a minstrel on the street, she sang a soft song until Mom rewarded her with a small dish of kibble.

On this particular day, after returning from her walk, I found Mom hunkered down in her office, click-click clicking away on her laptop. She didn't look up as I moseyed down the hall to the mudroom.

In the mudroom, I nibbled on a few nuggets of kibble but paused when fresh air drifted past my nose. As I lifted my nose toward the sweet smell, my eyes caught a ray of sunlight stretching across the floor. The sunshine streamed through an opening in the screen door, which stood ajar.

Mom had not closed it all the way.

I held my breath, tiptoed to the opening, and peeked out. Nothing waited outside to pounce on me. I pushed on the door. It eased open, then waited, tempting me to venture out.

My heartbeat quickened. I slipped through the crack, paused, and looked around. No, Mom tugged on my leash, trying to restrain me. I cast off my worries about aches and rusty joints and I bolted down the porch stairs. Around the side of the house, I ran until I picked up Wild Girl's scent and her secret path. Hardly an opening in the thick undergrowth, yet the path proved no secret to others. The thoroughfare carried dozens of scents of wild creatures. The aromas, like salmon rushing upriver, made me dizzy.

I stumbled along for a short distance before I stopped, crouched down on the trail, and caught my breath. A soothing hush, along with the smells, carried me back to many of the places I'd been from North Dakota to Louisiana and from Delaware to California. I whimpered with joy as I recalled the myriad of scents on my strolls along tree-covered paths or dry creek beds while I watched the evening shadows grow long. And oh, the people I met! The refrigerator repair man from Kalispell, Montana, told me about his cats, Lewis and Clark. The snowbirds from Canada who thought I was cool. And what about all my boondocking snowbirds I met in sunny Quartzite, Arizona? They were professors and truck drivers and widows and divorcees. Those from Montana or Idaho came not just to escape the winter, but also with the sole purpose of returning home with a golden tan that was the envy of their friends and family. And others would never go home because they came to the desert to escape lives that no longer worked for them.

As I crouched there on the path, the warm rays warmed my bones. I thought about who I had been... once a kitten with a family and now a lost and found cat.

A butterfly danced by, distracting me from my reverie. The Monarch's black and yellow wings brushed like a feather against my ear. I flicked my ear as another tickled my nose. I followed their flight as they flitted over to a patch of clover where they joined their swarm.

Image by image the past floated by until my heart, like it always did in this mood, locked onto its favorite scene... another wild girl from long ago. My Petunia. Together we chased those yellow clouds. The memory stirred up the cluster of butterflies that lived in my tummy.

My eye caught on a sunny patch where the long grass lay flat from the dew's weight. I sauntered toward the alluring spot and sat down. My fur still carried a sheen in the sunlight. I scoffed off my worries of growing old and preened. When finished, I curled up, inhaled a deep breath of fresh air, and fell asleep.

CHAPTER TEN

I don't know how long I dozed, but a familiar "mew-mew" woke me. My eyes popped open. Wild Girl sat nearby. I met her stare but braced to make a run for it.

Her jungle eyes gave me a long, slow blink. Again, the butterflies in my stomach. Shivers slid down my spine and crawled up my tail. With her front paw, she pointed to a small bird sleeping at her feet. She nudged it closer toward me and mewed again. When I only sat and stared, she picked up the small creature in her mouth, and stepping closer, dropped it at my feet. I studied the sleeping bird now right under my nose. What the...?

Not a sleeping bird! A dead bird! I backed away. Eeew!

The carcass lay under my nose. Had she killed it? Was she threatening me? Outrageous thoughts raced through my mind. Mom had warned me to stay away from the feral cats. I spun around and burst back down the path. Thorns scratched my face, as I pushed through the Blackberry bushes.

Squinting from their sting, I skidded to a stop. A long-ago image of Petunia came to mind. She blinked at me with her big golden eyes and pointed her nose at her feet where she had deposited the spoils of her hunt, a dead mouse, which she had offered in friendship.

I choked back a heat of humiliation as the reality of the situation with Wild Girl dawned on me. The dead bird was a gift. I growled with embarrassment. I had acted foolishly. Wild Girl only wanted to be friends… or more? The last thing I needed was another heartache. I've experienced enough in my lifetime.

I looked back over my shoulder. She padded up behind me, the dead bird in her mouth. I glared at her and her gift. Opening my mouth to hiss, the sound caught in my throat.

A raccoon lunged from the foliage. Angry-red eyes zeroed in on me from behind his masked face. He reared up. His claws raked the air and his bright-white teeth glinted like blades.

I stood in place, stunned. Before I could catch my breath, Wild Girl dropped the dead bird and flew past me. She pounced on the coon taking him down as her angry screech rocked me to my toes. The two became a blurred tangle of fangs and claws roiling on the muddy path. The masked bandit cried out as he wriggled from Wild Girl's clutches and waddled away as fast as his short legs would carry him.

Wild Girl belted out a final lioness roar while I remained like a stump without letting out even as much as a whimper. When the vegetation swallowed up the coon, Wild Girl turned to me.

Finally, I squeaked out a feeble chirp and hung my head. Unable to meet her eyes, I too, hurried down the path in the coon's wake without looking back. Luck led me out of the bramble and onto the paved walkway leading to the stairs. Taking the steps three at a time, I reached the door and slinked through the opening. Racing down the hall, to the bedroom I skidded under the bed.

I cowered there, concentrating on the click-clacking of Mom's computer until my heartbeat returned to normal. Resting my head on my paws I let out a dejected sigh. Who am I kidding? After all these years, I haven't changed a bit. I am still the throwaway kitten who failed to help feed his family, still, the sorry cat Petunia had foolishly risked her life to rescue, and I am still cowering while another she-cat saves my sorry ass.

I sat up, bumping my head on the bed frame. Grrrr! Belly-crawling, I crept out from under the bed, padded into Mom's office, and sat beside her chair. I mewed and gave her my most pathetic look which worked so well on her.

"Hey, little man. What have you been up to all morning?"

If I could talk, I would NOT confess I'd been outside alone. She never wanted me outside without her, and never without my harness and leash. But what I *would* tell her is that I hate the nickname she calls me, "Little Man."

She rolled her chair back and patted her lap. "Well, come on up here."

Sitting on Mom's lap always cheered me up. I mewed again.

"What? You want me to pick you up?" As she reached down to scoop me up a cloud of sadness flitted across her face. "Are your old bones aching? I know it's getting too hard to jump. Sometimes I feel the same way." Trying to mask her worry she planted an overexuberant sloppy kiss on my nose and hugged me. "You're the best cat ever."

Not really, but I liked that she thought so. Or did she? Her computer dinged, and she turned her attention back to it. She clicked her mouse and a woman's face filled the laptop's screen. Totally distracted, Mom focused her full attention on the woman.

And not me.

CHAPTER ELEVEN

"Carol! Hello, my friend! It's been a long time. How are you?"

The woman's lopsided smile lifted only one corner of her mouth. "I'm sorry. Life gets in the way. I'm doing okay."

Mom gave the woman one of her radiant smiles. "I haven't heard from you for a while. What have you been up to?"

Carol's expression warped yet she let out a chuckle. I thought she might cry.

"My Dad passed away last month. I've been busy taking care of things."

Mom's smile vanished and her attitude transformed into wrinkles of concern. "What? I'm so sorry. When? You should have called. I would have come back and helped; you know? Do you need anything?"

"No, I'm fine. The memorial was last month." The half-smile again. "I'm hanging in there." Her words came reluctantly as if her tired, gravelly voice had dragged them out into the open. "You remember I moved in with Dad after my divorce, right?"

"Yes, I remember. Your mom had just died, and your dad needed help. The last time we talked you had moved in with him and the two of you were really getting to know one another." Mom gave her friend a warm smile. "You shared some of his cop stories with me. They were so funny they had me rolling on the floor laughing. And the ones about the people whose lives he'd changed because of his bravery? They blew me away. Even though I never met him, I came to love him, too. I'm so sorry I never got to meet him."

Carol's eyes glistened as she held back her tears. Her smile returned but with a grimness. "Thanks. Moving in with him was the best thing I could have done. Although at the time I didn't think so." She rolled her eyes and the corner of her mouth turned downward. "Tom had divorced me. I had nowhere to go. So, I crawled back home with the excuse Dad needed help. Of course, he wouldn't admit it. I thought going home was the last straw in my pitiful life."

Mom nodded with an understanding grin. "I know the divorce was hard on you, but it ended up being so good for you. That time with your dad was precious. And what a place to land, right? Your folk's ranch is like a secluded oasis, just a mile from the city and yet so private."

Carol's eyes darted to the scene from her window. Her face softened. "Yes, I love it here." She turned back to her computer screen. "Looking back, everything happened just as it was supposed to." She gave Mom a lopsided grin. "Mom dying when she did. My negligent sisters never stepped up to help or even visit him. "The divorce…" she sighed. "It was all for the best. Yes, I'm thankful for the time I spent with him. I got to know the man he was. And I began to see myself through his eyes. He kept reminding me how special he thought I was. It was such a healing time for both of us."

Mom gave her friend a knowing smile and nodded. "You were so lucky to have that time with him. You know me. I believe there are no mistakes in the world. Everything happens at exactly the right time." Mom gave her friend a smirk and a weak chuckle. "But life sure has its twists and turns, doesn't it?" Mom flopped back in her chair and found her radiant smile and added. "So, what's next?"

Licking the emotional tears that had gathered on her lip, Carol hung her head. "I don't know. I'm trying to put on a brave front."

Mom brightened. "I've no doubt you'll get through this. I know it's hard, though. I've been where you are. But you're tough, like me. You'll get through this."

"I guess so. But there's more." Carol eyed Mom sideways with a nervous smile. "My sisters and their families have been a big problem."

Mom sat back up, leaning her elbows against her desk. "Oh no. That's too bad. You remember what I went through when *my* sister was dying? I can relate." Carol nodded.

I had been sitting quietly on Mom's lap listening to the two women catch up. I remembered Mom dealing with her sister's family when her sister was dying.

The memory stirred a flush of irritation. I sat up. Mom and her sister had been best friends. It was tragic when her sister's family began criticizing my mom's caregiving. The way they treated my mom was inexcusable. I would have spit at them if they'd come around me. She was already so sad about losing her best friend and sister. I watched Mom fade a little more every day as if she were dying too. She would come home, pick me up, hold me tight, and cry as she held me. I never complained how her tears soaked my fur.

Carol nodded again. "Dad became depressed after Mom died. Reasonably so, right? After sixty years of marriage?" The question was rhetorical. She didn't wait for an answer. "He started losing weight and my sisters didn't think I was taking good care of him. They insisted on hiring caregivers."

"Did that help? Did he start to eat better?"

Deflated, Carol shook her head. "The caregivers wanted to give him drugs for his depression, but he refused. He argued. 'The hurt reminds me of how much I loved your mom. Without the hurt, it's as if she didn't exist.'"

Carol's face brightened at the memory. Her smile warmed, soothing her pained expression. "Dad ended up consoling *me*. 'Hurt is just the other side of love,' he told me. And then he laughed to lighten my mood and begin singing. 'You know? Like love and marriage. You can't have one without the other.'" Carol laughed at her memory with a lopsided grin. "Another of Dad's wise sayings."

"Well, that's his right, isn't it? Not to take the meds if he doesn't want to?"

Carol raised her brows and nodded again. "Yes. I was fine with his decision. Sure, he'd lost weight. But jeez, I got depressed after my divorce, and my marriage didn't come close to sixty years."

"My sisters said I should be doing more. I argued with them." Her voice increased in volume. "I mean, I can't *make* him eat, right?" She kept fiddling with something off-camera. Her eyes darted back and forth and finally focused back on the computer screen. "They called in social services and started talking about elder abuse. They insisted he go to a care facility so he could get the 'proper care.'" Carol rocked sharply in her chair. "I was scared for him. And so angry at my sisters, at the system, and just everything."

Caught up in her friend's story Mom nervously tapped her foot. "What did you do?"

"I called an old friend I used to work with at child protection services. She helped me get an injunction against my sisters." Carol shook her head. "It's s a blessing he died when he did. We had a court date coming up. I'm hoping they'll just drop everything, but I worry they might still come after me. I'm scared."

Mom's shoulders drooped as she shook her head in disbelief.

Off-screen, Carol rapped a pencil or something against her desk. Her face warped in frustration and worry. "You know how it is these days. Dope 'em up. Being 'Blah' is the new norm." Finally, she sighed and cleared her throat. She rubbed away the wetness on her cheeks and then looked out her window. "This place has been my recluse. Dad had let everything go when he was taking care of Mom. I've enjoyed fixing it up. It's been my therapy. There are so many childhood memories here." She let out a long sigh.

I followed Carol's line of sight.

CHAPTER TWELVE

A tinge of familiarity flitted through me. The branches of two mimosa trees shaded freshly painted steps leading up to the porch. Had Carol replaced the unstable rotting wooden ones I remembered? The porch had been warped, gray, and bare of any paint at all, and an overgrowth of shrubbery surrounded it.

The neglected deck now bragged about the loving attention Carol had bestowed on it. Black glossy paint covered the railing's rusted iron. Two bright yellow rocking chairs listed lazily on the shiny porch flooring and the expansive, deep green lawn reminded me of a man's crewcut. The shrubbery stood tight and firm at attention. Was this the place where I had sniffed every overgrown blade of grass, searching for a clue of that might tell me where my family had gone?

"My sisters insist on selling the place." She frowned. "I don't have the money to buy them out."

Mom stopped jiggling her foot and gave her friend a reassuring smile. "Change is always hard. I wish I were there. I'd give you a big hug." Then Mom's voice took on a cheery note. "Maybe it's time for a new adventure? Some excitement! You could move here."

Carol's mood lightened. She made one last swipe at her wet cheeks and straightened her shoulders. "Thanks for listening. I needed a 'feel-good' pep talk fix from my friend." She laughed in disbelief. "Move to Oregon? Wow! Now that would be a *big* change!" She forced a bright smile at the thought. The idea of moving to Oregon flooded over her like when the surf hits the beach. And the last of the girlfriend's moodiness was washed out to the sea.

Carol beamed with cheery energy. "So, how're things going with you, my friend? I saw on Facebook you're moved into your new place." "Are you loving it?"

Mom followed her friend's change of tact. Returning Carol's resilient smile with one of her own Mom gazed around the room. "Yes, I am very happy." She rolled her chair aside so the camera could pick up the view of the room. "This is my office. Where it all happens, right? I absolutely love it here. It's so quiet and peaceful. I'm surrounded by nature." She turned the computer so that it faced the window. "There are trees everywhere you look. Deer graze in my yard. They like to eat rose bushes and hydrangeas, but that's an easy trade-off, don't you think? See the river across the street? And the ocean's only three miles down the road." Mom caught her breath.

Carol's red swollen eyes grew large as she stared at the ribbon of a river weaving its way through the green and gold background of pines, redwoods, and maples. In contrast, deep blue clouds floated above the pines. "Wow. My blood pressure went down ten points just looking at the view from here."

"Imagine what it would feel like if you were here! I keep asking myself, 'How lucky can a girl be?' I'm in shock that I've landed here. Out of all the places I've been, the universe brought me here. I'm overwhelmed. It's so easy to forget the craziness going on in the world." As she talked, Mom angled her laptop, so she could see Carol again. Out of breath, Mom flopped back in her chair.

My ears perked at the image on Carol's screen. Carol cradled a beautiful long-haired cat in her arms.

"Who do you have there?

Carol's features softened as she ran her hand over the back of a fluffy blond cat purring on her lap. "Meet Scarlett Petunia." She kissed a black smudge on the blonde bombshell's pillowy cheek. A bit of leftover dinner? The lovely creature closed her eyes. She seemed to smile as if her mom's affection calmed some storm in her heart.

A black smudge?

I caught my breath. My old heart sped up as a whimper escaped. Hearing my cry, the cat became alert. Scarlett Petunia's amber eyes scanned each side of where Carol sat and behind her as if looking for the source of my cry. Then she pointed her ears at the laptop's screen.

Carol held Scarlett Petunia so that her pet faced the computer's camera lens. "You remember Petunia, don't you?" Petunia and Carol filled Mom's computer screen.

"Isn't she the cat you found living under your dad's porch?"

"Yep, this is her." She pecked a kiss on top of Petunia Scarlet's' head. "She was sick, and cold and hungry when I took her in. She had this ugly oozing wound. She looked like she'd been through a war of her own. At that time in my life, I could relate. My insides felt like what she looked like on the outside." Carol's eyes crinkled at the corners. "I named her Scarlett Petunia. I call her Petunia for short."

Mom chuckled. "Of course. *The Gone with the Wind* theme. Your favorite movie. I remember."

Carol grinned sheepishly. "Yes, I always wanted to name a cat after Scarlett Ohara. As luck would have it, when I found her, she was lying in an overgrown bed of Petunias. And guess what? They were a deep crimson variety. So, the name had to be Scarlett Petunia."

"I remember. She was such a scrawny stray. She's not the same cat. She's beautiful." Mom rocked back in her chair as she studied the cat on the computer.

"You were always rescuing cats. What happened to that mama cat and her litter of kittens you rescued? It was right before I got Sportster and before you rescued Scarlet, wasn't it? Do you still have them?"

"It was before you got Sportster. Remember, I asked you if you wanted one of the kittens?" Carol paused. She gave Mom a teasing smirk and raised her brow. "You told me you didn't like cats." The tilt of her head matched her lopsided smile. "Remember?"

I looked at Mom. I had heard Mom tell others how she didn't like cats until she had me. Sometimes that knowledge made me feel special but other times I felt I was a charity case, and the day would come when she would tire of me. Mom gave her friend her lopsided grin. "I didn't *know* I liked cats."

"The kittens were undernourished, and the mama cat had festering sores from fighting. I only kept them long enough to nurse them back to health, then had them neutered and spayed."

"You've always had a soft spot for dogs and cats and birds. Any lost or hurt critter. Your dad did too. You were always telling me about some creature he had taken in that needed a home."

Carol's expression softened. "Yep. Dad was like that, too. Most were sick or injured and he knew if he called the Humane Army, they would probably just put them down. Many of his rescues became barn cats after he nursed them back to health and they lived to be an old age."

I let out a harrumph. "Humane? I think not. The nice-nice name was only a cover. They were a ruthless bunch." I shivered. I wondered if my family had been lucky enough to be rescued from the grasp of the People's Humane Army by someone like Carol and her dad.

I jumped onto the desk, sat in front of the laptop, and stared at the screen. Carol's Scarlett Petunia looked directly at me. My heart lodged in my throat. I let out a long, guttural caterwaul.

CHAPTER THIRTEEN

Carol had not adopted just some stray! Scarlett Petunia? I think not. The cat on the screen was *my Petunia*! She was not dead. She was alive and well!

Mom pushed me off the desk and onto her lap and pinned me in her lap. "Sportster, you're in the way. What's gotten into you?"

Carol's Scarlett Petunia rubbed against the corner of her mom's computer screen with closed eyes. A dainty trilling chirp, like a birdsong, escaped her tiny mouth in answer to my lovesick call.

Once more, I twisted out of Mom's arms and climbed back onto the desk. I rubbed my chin hard against the corner of Mom's laptop screen. My chin met only hard plastic, and the computer began to fold close. Startled, my eyes popped open. Before I could figure out what happened to Petunia, Mom grabbed me again. This time, deep lines creased her forehead and her eyes narrowed to slits. "Sportster!" She shoved me forcefully back onto her lap. Her left arm squeezed me so tight I could hardly breathe. With her free hand, she flipped the laptop back open.

Petunia's eyes grew big and round, and she let loose a series of trilling chirps in answer to my lovesick call. I couldn't help myself. I sprang back onto the desk.

Carol giggled. "I think they like each other."

Did this Scarlet Petunia recognize me? Doubts intruded. Maybe she's only a reflection. Once again, I wiggled from Mom's grasp, jumped up on the desk, and planted my rump in front of the laptop.

And again, I howled. This time like the mountain lion I'd heard in the Wyoming backcountry when he called out to his mate. His keen wail not only carried across the countryside shattering the silent night, but it also sent a shock right through me.

And once again, Mom whisked me away, this time replanting me on the floor. "Sportster! What's wrong with you?"

I growled under my breath as my paws touched the ground. And you better believe it! I sprang right back onto the desk and climbed over her arm, even as she tried to shove me aside.

My Petunia, or Carol's Petunia, whoever, rubbed her chin against the corner of her mom's computer. That adorable beauty smudge on her cheek filled the edge of Mom's screen. The furry mark appeared softer and her nose a brighter pink than I remembered. I stretched my chin toward her and closed my eyes in hopes that I might nuzzle her.

My teeth scraped the corner of the screen, rattling me back to reality. My eyes flew open. I found myself grinding my chin against the hard plastic corner of Mom's laptop, which almost poked my eye out.

I'd been sucker-punched. Petunia, Scarlett, or whoever, she was only an illusion like the images on the TV screen. A long sad moan for my lost love escaped from its prison deep inside me, where I had kept it contained for so many years.

I moaned again. And again! Out of my mind with embarrassment and startled by my lack of control, I flew off the desk and sped from the room. I had to get away. I raced not to the bedroom and under the bed; it was not far enough. I bound down the hall, skidded around the corner, and slid into the mudroom. Still ajar, the screen door leered at me. I bolted outside.

Down the deck stairs, past the garden patio, I scrambled, and dove into the tunnel opening in the blackberry bushes. Through blinding emotions, I thought I had buried deep in a hole and covered up, broke loose. I ran, and I ran so fast that even the rabbits couldn't catch me.

I ran as fast as I could, but the memories clung on like ticks. They would not let go. Now free from their imprisonment, they bombarded my sensibilities. Unable to fight off the age-old scenes they took over my being.

Petunia and I rolled and tumbled in the long grass that tickled our noses and ear. We pranced around and pranced on one another until sweet exhaustion overtook us and we collapsed in the warm sunshine, curling up and snuggling together; our purring soothed us to sleep. We slept until cool darkness woke us. My innocence offered up a fairy tale story, and I quickly made my own. She loved me. I was her Tom, and the world was mine.

I shook my head to clear the cobwebs of the past. When Petunia had disappeared so long ago, confusing voices had hammered inside my head making me dizzy. Now they were back. *Who are you kidding? Do you think she just disappeared?* Distraught my gut knotted up. I couldn't answer.

No one ever stays, you fool. Why would she be any different? She didn't vanish; she left you. She grew tired of your immaturity. Why would she stay?

With renewed strength, the voices of doubt thundered inside my head. The possibility Petunia might have left on purpose was still unbearable to face.

In the past, my pride had mercifully stepped up offering the scenario that Petunia had died. And without shame, I seized that possibility. I embraced the pompous but plausible story. She had crawled away to save me the heartache of my finding her dead from her wounds... the wounds she never would have suffered from if I had protected her.

But that was the past. Now, out of breath and panting I collapsed at the edge of the clearing. So, who was that in Mom's computer? Petunia's ghost? Had she come to haunt me? Or had she come for me? Is it my time to die?

I sat up, cleaned the wet grass from my paws, and pulled the stickers from my fur. The gurgling song of the brook and the wind in the maples weakened my tormented thoughts. My heartbeat slowed. Feeling foolish but better, I wondered. How could one she-cat still have such an effect on me? A leaf floated to the ground. I pounced on it, making it crackle. I stalked around for another distraction trying to get lost in my mindless game until… I balked.

CHAPTER FOURTEEN

I came up short, almost bumping into Wild Girl. She must have been watching me from the edge of the clearing. I backed away from her. She looked different. Not like the homeless cat that she was. She poised like an Egyptian Queen. I wanted to look more closely but resisted. Turning away, I pretended to be engrossed in my game of seeking another crunchy leaf to pounce upon. When I did chance another look, she had not moved. Still confident and composed, she sat like a Sphinx guarding her kingdom. And watched me.

I raised my tail straight up and with a dismissive air into the air resumed my playful bravado while quickly making my way back up the path, to the house, and to Mom.

✾ ✾ ✾ ✾ ✾

I found Mom in her office, finishing up the call from her friend. "It was great catching up. When things get settled, I hope you'll visit. I would love to show you around. This would be a great place to regroup."

"That sounds like a plan. It's so beautiful there. I already feel rejuvenated. "

"Give Scarlett Petunia a big hug from me… and from Sportster, too." They both clucked like a couple of hens over a new rooster as I landed on Mom's lap.

Carol wrapped her arms around her Scarlett. Kissing and hugging her she gushed. "And this hug's from Sportster."

Carol's Petunia leaned in for her mom's expected kiss but caught sight of me when I climbed up on Mom's lap. Her golden orbs widened, and she homed in on me. Her purring rose to a crescendo matching my heart's vibration pounding in my chest. If she's a ghost…

Like a rutting elk, I exhaled a deep moan.

Mom and Carol cackled even louder.

"Do we have the beginnings of a budding romance?" Mom's grin spread wide across her face. Raising her brow, she ruffled my fur and looked back at her friend on the screen. "Now, you *have to* visit." I jiggled as Mom laughed heartily. "If you don't, Scarlett and Sportster will never forgive you."

Carol's mood had lightened, smoothing the lines on her forehead. She appeared younger. The crook at the corner of her mouth turned upward as she bent down and pecked several more kisses on Scarlett's cheek.

My Petunia twisted away, ignoring her mother's affections, and proceeded to rub up against their computer again. Petunia's adorable face filled our screen. So lifelike… for a ghost.

Carol smiled at Mom and me. "It's been great catching up, my friend. You always brighten my day. I'll get back to you after the house sells."

"Same here, girlfriend. If you need anything, let me know."

The screen faded to black. My Petunia was gone. Again.

Mom sighed, closing her laptop. Her gaze drifted to the scene outside the window, and she drew in a deep breath. "Why don't we go outside? It's a beautiful day, Sportster. You can catch some rays while I read."

After snagging my harness on and snapping on my leash Mom grabbed her book and led me outside. On the patio, she stretched out on the lounge chair. I joined her taking my place at her feet.

The sun warmed my bones as I took in the green landscape. Mr. Blue Jay chattered a hello and carried on about what a great day it was. I let my mind wander.

What if the Petunia in Mom's computer is not a ghost? What if she lives and breathes? A shiver of excitement trickled down my spine to my tail. I went over every detail of our computer encounter.

The computer screen disclosed more than just Carol and Petunia. When Carol gazed out her window, the unnerving coincidences of its view rattled me.

Two flowering mimosa trees. I remembered them. A porch framed by a black-iron railing. The same porch. The only difference? Glossy black paint instead of rusted iron on the railing. Another difference. Crisp dandelion yellow paint covered the rockers once warped gray wood that I remembered. Could it be the same forgotten porch from my past, now lovingly restored?

I sat up and glanced at Mom. Her book lay flat on her chest, and she slept. Inhaling the Christmas scent of the surrounding pines, the aroma tingled my nose. As if on cue to ruin the peaceful setting, two blackbirds cawed from atop the woodshed, cutting into my reverie. Their claws grated across the tin roof, disturbing the quiet. Could they be the same vexing birds that lived in the Mimosa trees in my past? Talk about coincidences. Birds migrate. But probably not. I'm sure there are plenty of these damning varmints here in Oregon. I spat out a strong curse in their direction.

What had happened to Petunia back then? What if she's still alive? Maybe she had just got up and left? After all, my dad left, my real mom left, and my siblings too.

How could Carol's Petunia be attracted to me if she's not real? She's only an image on the TV screen, right? And yet, although it made no sense, I couldn't shake the feeling. *I knew* she was real. Is the cat on Mom's computer screen? The one Carol calls Scarlett Petunia? She's *my* Petunia.

Maybe what I saw on the computer was just wishful thinking on my part. Ghosts can appear as if they're real, can't they? I stood up and tried to shake off the unending questions haunting me. What was wrong with me? I had given Petunia up for dead a long time ago. Why can't I let dead cats lie?

Like the blackbirds, the questions continued to haunt me. What if The People's Humane Army cat-knapped my Petunia? They had probably taken my mom and my siblings, too.

Dad and Grandpa had always warned us. "Be aware of the People's Army. They kill wild cats." Dad and Grandpa went on to explain the Army's preaching. "Wild cats live a lonely, cruel, and harsh life. They can't be rehabilitated. The needle is the only humane thing to do." They reminded me that the Army was everywhere. I remembered Mom hiding us from them. So, if I'm right and that's true, and they took her, then Petunia is dead. They're all dead.

I had locked these disturbing questions in a deep corner of my brain for years. But now they had erupted their stinking heads from the litter box where I had buried them. I jerked my head around. Still rapping and raking their claws on the woodshed's tin roof, the annoying blackbirds renewed their incessant cawing as if giving me some sick high-five. They wouldn't let up.

Carol's Petunia might really be my Petunia. No one wants a sick and injured cat, and yet Carol said she'd rescued her "Scarlett Petunia, who *was* sick and injured. Had she saved my Petunia from the Army?

But again, who would want a sick and injured cat? Maybe Petunia collapsed that day before she had reached the den. She could have passed out from her weak condition and lay in the open, vulnerable, and near death.

I should never have encouraged her to go hunting with me that day. Should ofs and could ofs, I couldn't make any sense of it. I stood, circled around, seeking a cushier spot, and flopped back down. The questions wouldn't stop. Is she dead or alive?

Go back home. Find out.

What? No! The idea of a long, solo journey frightened me as much as thinking Petunia was a ghost. I shuddered at the thought. I'm older and wiser now. I can no longer bolster my courage with my foolish, youthful mantra, Activate Lion Mode. Sure, it helped me through my Olympic Forest adventure. But the accident had forced that adventure upon me. I had no choice.

But now? If I took on the quest... I groaned. There would be close encounters. Predators. The worst kind. The human ones who think they know best. And always those vexing blackbirds, taunting me at every curve in the path. No, I'm not going to kid myself. Activating lion mode was no longer practical.

But as I look back, the Olympic adventure proved anything was possible if you Activate Lion Mode. Do I still believe that? I don't know. Had it been courage that spurred me on, or my youthful bravado? Am I too old? I had to consider everything. I shook my head. I'm not dead yet.

But leaving Mom? Could I do that? We have been through so much together. She needs me. And yet, as I recall those days lying on that porch alongside Petunia, peeling paint from her fur. The memories call to me.

Blocking out the blackbirds' cawing and cawing and cawing I thought of one of those summer days... the sun warmed us as we watched the Mimosa fronds sway in the breeze... I drifted away.

CHAPTER FIFTEEN

I jerked awake. Long shadows stretched across the patio pavers. Mom still slept. Her calming presence reminded me that in all these years she's always been there for me. Except for the accident in the forest when I couldn't help but watch the People's Humane Army carry her away while she slept. But she had escaped and searched for me until she found me. For the first time, I felt like someone cared.

And yet, what unthinkable thoughts was I thinking? Leaving her? How could I? Lately, even when she only went shopping for a couple of hours, I suffer the desperate and humiliating insecurity of old age. I wait shamelessly at the door until she returns, and then I call her out for her neglect.

Sure, I have always met her at the door complaining, but back then they were hollow complaints. She needed to be reassured, to know I cared. These days are different. The anxiety of age sometimes takes control and exposes me.

I climbed onto her chest and laid my paw gently on her cheek to wake her. Her eyes fluttered open. Her sleepy expression melted into a warm smile. "Hello, my little man. I guess I dozed off." She blinked in the long rays of the afternoon sun.

I leaned in as she scratched my ears and chin.

"What do you need, little buddy?" She closed her book and checked the time on her phone. "It's getting late. We'd better go in." But she didn't get up. Instead, she scratched my back and drew me close, laying kisses all over my face, and rubbing her nose against mine. Instead of pulling away, I revved up my purring.

CHAPTER SIXTEEN

Mom carried me inside, patted me, and sat me down. I padded to my food dish, checked it, and then scurried past the French doors heading toward Mom's office.

Wild Girl lay soaking up the last rays of sunshine. She lifted her head as I passed. I didn't acknowledge her but kept on track and hurried into Mom's office. Hopping onto her empty office chair, and onto the desk, I planted my rear on top of the closed laptop where I proceeded to lick and preen… and wait.

In the kitchen, the microwave hummed, then dinged. The pine wood floor creaked under Mom's stockinged footfall, announcing Mom's approach. She entered the room clutching a steaming mug of coffee in one hand and a notebook in the other.

Setting her brew on the desk, she picked me up and set me aside on the nearby barrel chair which she called *my chair*. "You know I don't like you sitting on my computer."

I remained where she had set me until she settled into her seat at her computer. When the screen lit up, I leaped from my position to the desk and began rubbing against the laptop's screen.

"Sportster! You're blocking my view." She pushed me away.

I climbed over her arm determined to continue my vigilance.

"No." She snatched me up again, this time not so gently, and dropped me roughly to the floor.

I hissed. She stiffened. Then glared at me. "I don't know what's gotten into you, but you'd better watch."

But before the last words, 'that attitude,' left her lips, I had already sprung back onto the desk and was sitting next to the computer. I bellowed out a heartfelt moan. And again, I rubbed my chin hard against the laptop's lid until it snapped shut.

She reached for me. "I said no!"

This time, ears pinned against my head, I growled and swatted her hand. Without claws, I couldn't hurt her, but she knew what I meant.

She scowled at me. I held my breath and met her hard eyes with a mean look of my own. I dared her to challenge me one more time.

Her old-time clock ticked, ticked, ticked. The thin line of her lips slowly curled at the corners. Her face softened. "I'm sorry, Sportster. I don't know what your problem is, but you can't talk to me that way." She scratched my chin. "You can sit here but quit pushing on the screen."

I relaxed my ears and gave her a long, slow blink, wishing I could explain what I was going through. Because of *him*, I knew Mom would understand. She had been where I am now.

I first met *him* when he stood outside our motorhome's door. Before Mom invited him in, I knew he would change things. By the time he reached the top step, the energy spit and sparked between the two, like wild cats in heat. When he stepped inside, like two cats sizing up one another, they took neutral corners. He sat on the couch. Mom sank into her chair behind her desk. I perched in the overhead alcove and watched the scene unfold.

His lips formed a simper of a smile, not quite a grin, as he sized up Mom. I imagined he had coveted the affection for years, saving it only for Mom because it transformed him. He lit up behind his barrier of thick whiskers and his eyes sparkled with childish mischief. "It's been a long time," he said.

I am only a cat, but I knew this was what they called a life-changing moment. They spoke with great restraint as they fought the electric tension that charged the space between them. Mom sat on the edge of her chair. Her breathing came in small puffs as she feigned calmness she didn't feel. They talked small talk, like children wading in the river, testing the waters.

And then, he tensed. The smallest of movements. I don't think Mom noticed. He'd decided to take the dive, whether the water was cold or not.

"Can I just kiss you?" The words hung in the air between them, fizzing like the lit fuse of Wylie Coyote's dynamite in a Road Runner cartoon.

Mom let out the breath she'd been holding. I held mine. Time stopped.

We waited. He and I. I wanted to cheer her on. Surely, she would not refuse. I didn't think she could. An alluring enchantment penetrated every particle of air. The same enchantment overcame me when I was near Petunia.

The love mode.

I tucked away the memory that wasn't even mine. Returning to 'my' chair I curled up between the pillows. I wouldn't push it. Tomorrow was another day. If I had words—but of course I don't— I would explain my outlandish actions. Now it was of no use. And anyway, I had no proof Petunia was even real. Maybe she was just a creation of my imagination. After all, what we had experienced happened long ago. We were so young.

A musical dream about love lost floated in the air like a sad country song. The low beat of a guitar twanged, its resonance tickling my whiskers. I scrunched into a tighter ball. The melody continued, this time its vibrations itched my ear, and I flicked it.

When the third annoyance woke me, I shook my head, blinked in the darkness, and sat up, trying to clear the fog of fantasies. Mom had gone to bed. Moonbeams from the window cast shadowy shapes across the floor. Caught in the glow of the moody light a pair of emerald orbs glowed in front of my chair. I balked.

"Mew." It was *her* again.

I held back a myriad of reactions. And hissed. I didn't want to wake Mom. What was she doing in my house? I braced to run.

Seeing I was awake she whispered another "Mew," and flopped to the floor. She rolled onto her back. Twisting and switching her tail she purred a gurgling and alluring song.

How did she get in? Mom must have let her in. A rush of anger surged through me. How could Mom do this to me? I glared at Wild Girl like an indignant father with his arms crossed and tapping his foot. My tail thumped steadily against the chair's arm.

No reaction. I straightened, raised my tail high like a cavalryman riding into battle, and leaped over her gyrating body. I intended to get to the bottom of this. Landing with a grunt, I trotted down the dark hall to check the door. I didn't look back but grumbled louder when Wild Girl padded behind me like a shadow.

First, I checked the door. Closed tight. She hadn't accidentally got in. Mom had let her in. That really ruffled my fur. Second, I sniffed my food and water bowls. Still full.

Wild Girl eased closer. I hissed over my shoulder and spat out a warning for her to keep her distance. This was too much. Did she think she could eat my food too? Just because Mom had taken her in, it didn't mean she had free rein here. I glared at my dishes and growled again. I'll have to guard them all night. I cursed Mom.

With my back to Wild Girl, I dropped down on my haunches, and like a sphinx, guarded my possessions. Wild Girl waited for an invitation that was never going to come from me. Finally, she voiced another of her pathetically meek mews and turned away. Good. With a delicate but too-confident gait, she tiptoed back down the hall.

What!? Where's she going now? She'd better not be crawling in bed with Mom. That was never going to happen either!

I skidded around the corner, catching up with her as she entered Mom's bedroom. My hair on end, my tail rigid, I shoved my way between her and Mom's bed. But she had already rounded the foot of the bed and was entering the walk-in closet. If she thought she was going to curl up in the clothes basket…

I scrambled toward the closet. Slipping and sliding on the knotty pine floor, I skidded into the area rug scrunching it into a pile. But I regained my balance. I burst into the dark closet, skidded to a stop, and balked again.

Wild Girl was gone.

CHAPTER SEVENTEEN

Was she a ghost too? I poked around the clothes and checked the laundry basket to make sure she wasn't hiding there. I sniffed the air… only tennis shoes and lavender laundry soap… and fresh air? I sniffed again.

I spotted the source, an open window above the closet dresser. I studied the window until my neck ached. The peace of the late hour was deceiving. The window's smiling gap jeered and taunted me. I spat at the situation like a boy whistling in the dark.

What happened here? I took on the task of washing my face, my tail, and then my paws. The mindless chore helped to purge my confusion. A cool draft drifted down on the cool night breeze. I caught Wild Girl's scent.

Was that Wild Girl's escape hatch?

I glanced over my shoulder. Mom still lay sleeping. She had not let Wild Girl in. I sent her an unspoken apology for doubting her loyalty to me.

I found myself perched on top of the dresser; my paws braced on the windowsill. When I nudged my nose against the screen for a better view, to my surprise it gave way. Poking my head through, I looked down.

Ten feet below, Wild Girl sat on the walkway staring up at me. Our house, built on the side of the hill, appeared to be a bird's nest in the trees, but really it rested on ten-foot-high pillars. That's a long way down. How could she jump that far? Was she some kind of a super cat? Was she waiting for me to follow? I couldn't jump that far. But if I didn't, what would she think? Wild Girl let out one of her pathetic mews which was both irritating and endearing at the same time.

Like a satellite dish, her ears rotated back and forth homing in on every night sound. I knew the dangers in the wild. I knew who hunted who. I shivered. She seemed at ease, but her tail proved she was always on alert as it twitched tightly in cadence with her ears.

The bedcovers rustled. I pulled back inside. Mom turned over in her sleep. If she's waking up, I can't go. I wouldn't want her to worry. Anyway, how would I sneak back in? Mom lay still so I poked my head through the screen again.

A scraping noise interrupted the doubts hammering around in my head. Then something brushed against my cheek. Startled, I squeezed my eyes shut and tried to jerk my head back inside. In my panic, the screen snagged on my throat almost choking me. As I tried to wiggle from its grasp, another scraping sound, and then something struck my nose.

My eyes sprang open. My attacker was only a tree limb, swaying in the breeze. While scratching against the torn screen, it brushed its leaves back and forth across my face. Controlling an urge to cry out, a gave one last jerk and backed out of the window. I didn't want to wake Mom… and what would Wild Girl think?

The mystery was solved. Wild Girl was not a super cat. She must have used the tree branch as a walkway and then scurried down the trunk. I would not have to jump! Adrenaline filled me with newfound courage. Wild Girl must think I can make it. Why else was she waiting? Lightheaded, I quivered at the possibility of a night adventure with Wild Girl. Who better to explore the nightlife than with her? Petunia's memory poked her head out of the box where I kept it contained. I shoved it back inside.

I started to push through the window, but a thought stopped me. I hung my head. I don't have front claws, only back ones. Only a slight difficulty scurrying up a tree... but what about going down?

I growled, took a couple of deep breaths, and slowed my racing heartbeat. My clownish idea of exploring evaporated in a poof. So, what if I don't jump? What do I care what Wild Girl thinks? She's just a homeless cat.

CHAPTER EIGHTEEN

The buzz of Mom's alarm broke my reverie. I scrambled off the dresser, making a blundering landing. Stumbling I caught my balance, pushed aside my disappointment and exhaustion, and hopped up beside Mom. I sat on her pillow beside her head.

Her eyes remained closed, but a dreamy grin told me she was awake. Pulling the covers over her head she rolled away from me. I climbed over her body and pawed at the lump that was her face under the blanket. The alarm sounded again. She groaned. Eyes still closed she poked her head back out from under the covers. With a feather-light touch, I brushed my paw against her cheek. The tickle nudged her back to the present.

With her eyes half open she grabbed the phone and quieted its annoying buzzing. Stretching and yawning, she pulled me close. "What a wonderful way to wake up, with my main guy watching over me. You look so cozy and cuddly you make me want to sleep in." I pawed at her again. She reciprocated by kissing me. "Alright, alright, I'm getting up. Hugging me again and blubbered between more kisses, "I love you so much."

I puffed up with an indignant air and scoffed at her exuberance.

Stiffening, I twisted loose from her grasp. Her silliness made me tingly, but I would never admit it. After she sat up and dragged her sleepy body into the bathroom, I curled up on the warm spot she had left.

I watched as she went through her human version of a grooming routine.

She sat at her vanity making the final pokes and pulling at her hair and drawing lipstick on her mouth. Making a face, she clamped her lips together, gave her image in the mirror a satisfied look, and turned to me. "I've been thinking..."

Her gushiness always made me wonder about that first day when the man brought me to Mom's grooming shop. The man had called me a stray Why didn't she didn't send the man and me to the Peoples Humane Army shelter? A lot of people still call me a rescue. Like a kinder word makes a difference. Either way, it means the same. I was a cat no one wanted. But if I could, I would explain. I was neither a stray nor a rescue. I had a family. And I would have found them if no one had interfered and *rescued* me.

Other people wondered about me too. They asked how a dog groomer like Mom ended up with a cat. She always laughs and answers, "I never intended to own a cat. I didn't like cats. And now, I wouldn't have it any other way."

I let out a smug meow. The feeling was mutual. As if anyone ever owns a cat. I had not wanted to live with her either. I had only wanted to go home to my real mom and my siblings.

"I've been thinking," Mom said again as she grabbed her jeans from their hook and danced her funny jig as she slipped into them and zipped them up. "What if I load up the motorhome and we surprise Carol with a visit?"

I twitched my tail at the idea. "Really?" I caught my breath. "Wait! What do you mean, *I*? Don't you mean *we*?"

"Her place will sell fast. I could be ready to go down there and help her pack." Raising her brows, she broke out in a big grin. "And you can meet Scarlett."

I let out the breath I was holding. The butterflies stirred in my belly. "Oh ok. Now you're talking," I purred.

Slipping into her shoes, she checked her image in the mirror one last time and headed down the hall.

I bolted off the dresser, passed her up, and led her to the kitchen. Full of excitement I made a happy leap for the countertop but lost my footing on the edge and tumbled to the floor.

Mom rushed up behind me. "Oh, my poor baby. Here, I'll help you up." Her brow wrinkled as she set me on the counter and turned on a thin stream of water. 'I know that's what you want."

I ignored her worried look as I lapped at the steady stream. She forced a grin and with a voice a little higher than normal she added. "You and I are getting soft. We need to work out more. What do ya say?"

I gave her no mind. Licking my lips, I sat back and proceeded to wash my face. I missed the jump because I'd been distracted thinking about the road trip and meeting Scarlett… or Petunia. I would finally find out. Is she real or is she Scarlett? Or is she a ghost?

Each day Mom piled items onto the dining room table and took them to the motorhome. Each day I sat among the clothes and bags of personal items in case it might be the last load. If so, I wanted to make sure she didn't forget me.

But my traveling carrier, my food and water bowls, and my leash and harness remained in the mud room. As the days dragged by the hope of a road trip faded and my anxiety level rose. Was she going to leave me at home?

I couldn't shake the doubt. What was I even thinking? For someone who said she didn't like cats, why would she want to take me? I hated it even after all these years I worried if I belonged. I had forgotten what Mom had said to the man who had found me on the street. "It will be easy to find a home for such a cute little guy." I had waited and waited for her to give me away. Maybe I am still waiting.

I know I am a throw-away-cat, but I keep my chin up. I make nice with Mom and obey her rules. I tolerate the same food every day, the baths, the leash, and the harness. When she takes me outside, she limits the places I want to explore. She let them stick me with needles and I came home missing body parts. Be harmless, don't bite. Act young. Stay healthy. Add it all up. It's a steep price in exchange for a home. But I put up with the rules, so Mom spoils me with toys and tasty treats. That helps.

But when cats and even people don't toe the line? If we kick the traces, rebel, and cross over that invisible line marked in the sand? They retaliate. They separate the rebels, cut them from the herd... and take you to the shelter.

Mom pretty much thought like the others. She always warned me. "Stay away from the wild cats. They're hard to love and turn old and sickly before their time. They live without a litterbox. They're dirty. They sure don't eat Fancy Feast. They scrape to live off the land. and without vaccines or neutering, they're a danger to others." Then she hugs me and with a big kiss says, "You are one lucky cat, Sportster."

I know I'm privileged. I sleep in a warm bed out of the rain and the wind. I have time to play with my myriad of toys. And I eat and drink anytime I want, albeit the same food every day. I'm neutered, I've had my shots, and I'm even declawed. I'm harmless. I am clean and healthy, and I don't kick the traces, I follow the rules. But what if...? My mind went to the open window in the closet.

What if I do take the leap? Quit playing the waiting game? Give up the comforts? What if I break out on my own? Go wild? Be like Wild Girl. I spat at the air and hissed. Let everyone call me an underprivileged cat and a dirty danger. So, what?

I'll find Petunia.

CHAPTER NINETEEN

The next night, Wild Girl's loud and incessant meowing interrupted Mom and me as we watched TV. When I trotted over to the French door and peer through the glass panes s to investigate, I found her sitting proudly, like a child showing off her latest scribbled picture. The object of her excitement lay at her feet—a dead mouse.

My stomach almost retched at the thought of eating her food offering. I spat at her and growled at her suggestion. Pulling her attention away from her movie, Mom threw me a disapproving frown and came over to inspect. Upon seeing the corpse at Wild Girl's feet. She smiled down in adoration of the gift and opening the door she crooned. "Oh, look what a good hunter you are! Thank you very much for your offer, but we have enough food."

I hissed again, not at Wild Girl but at Mom's encouraging attitude. Meanwhile, Wild Girl ignored my opinion. She puffed her chest out and continued to mew proudly a few more times. Mom never touched the offensive gift but reassured Wild Girl. She was a wonderful hunter and then returned inside and shut the door.

The next morning, I woke up in a bad mood. Wild Girl's offering was gone, not a feather or a hunk of fur to be seen. She must have eaten the whole thing. The thought grossed me out, but Wild Girl's generosity to share her meal softened my crustiness. Unbeckoned, the butterflies stirred in my tummy. Again, I growled in annoyance.

Mom had not taken a load to the motorhome or mentioned the trip in over a week. Outside, Wild Girl sat sphinxlike, prim, and proper on the patio's doormat. Her soft front paws clicked together like a Marine at attention. Her tail curled over her toes. She had finished eating the last of the kibble and now gazed at the pond's waterfall dropping lazily over the rocks.

Tired of waiting for Mom to either announce whether the trip was on …or off. my irritation grew. I worried. I was not getting any younger. I kept my moments of confusion to myself. And my aching joints that made me miss my mark when I jumped. But I refused to become the hide-under-the-bed-cat. I might not be getting any younger, but I am not dead yet.

Wild Girl's escape hatch in the closet called out to me. This is your chance to make it up to Petunia. Prove yourself. I stretched, easing out the kinks in my joints, and headed for the kitchen. Acing the jump onto the counter, I sat at the edge of the sink. Yes! I'm not dead yet!

I waited for Mom to turn the faucet on.

Always waiting. Why were we staying so long here in this house anyway? What had become of our home on wheels? When Mom and I woke in it, every morning was a new location. We couldn't wait to go outside and explore. A lot of cats couldn't handle our vagrant lifestyle. But me? I loved it. It was food for my curiosity. Traveling made me feel alive! Everyone I met thought I was the coolest cat ever.

Campers gushed and poured their praises all over me. "Oh! I love your kitty! Can we pet him?!" Mom would smile and nod and they would drop to their knees and babble on usually about their cat whom they had left at home. "We have a cat too, but he hates to travel." Patting my head and scratching my ears they made over me like I was an Egyptian God. "Every time we try to take our Felix in the RV he bawls constantly. So, we have to leave him at home. We miss him so much." Mom beamed while I pretended to shrug off the attention.

*　*　*　*　*　*

I found myself on top of the closet dresser peering out the window. The pavers on the path below cast a wet shine in the moonlight proving a quiet rain had snuck in during the night and soaked the earth. Wild Girl was nowhere to be seen. No matter. My mind was made up. I was going to find Petunia. I could feel it in my bones. I had no doubts, no fear. She was all I ever wanted. Other cats dreamed of climbing the tallest trees or becoming like the *Lion King*. But me? I never wanted anything more than hunting, playing, and sleeping with Petunia.

For some reason, my mind flashed back to Mom and the man who had come to our motorhome. She did kiss him that day. It was more than a peck on the cheek. They kissed and kissed. Their energy flared up between them like lightning in the sky. I thought they might burn the place down. I jumped from my alcove and trotted over to them where they stood embracing. Standing on my hind legs, I pawed at Mom's thigh, begging her to pick me up. I wanted to be a part of the powerful, joyful force they had created together. But now I understand. I have to find my own connection. Mom had found hers. I had to find mine… with Petunia.

*　*　*　*　*　*

My pulse pounded against my temples as I waited until Mom slept soundly. When I thought I would burst if I waited any longer, I shoved my nose against the screen and crept out onto the limb. Boy, you can really breathe out here! The fresh scent of the rain stirred up an exhilaration inside of me. It seemed I could smell every leaf and flower in the whole world. I was on my way.

Was it my weight or the wind making the limb sway? I splayed my toes and hung on. I took a shaky step. Then another. And then, I burst across the branch. Each step became more solid as the branch grew wider. At the main trunk, I leaned against it, caught my breath, and waited for my heartbeat to slow.

I made the mistake of looking down.

My throat tightened. I cast a longing glance at the window. No! Don't look back! That's not an option. Anyway, the torn screen seemed a mile away. But the alternative…? My stomach roiled, but not with butterflies. They had transformed into angry bees.

I growled. Jerking my head around I concentrated on what stood between me and the ground. Branches of various thicknesses, like rungs on a ladder, led to the walkway below. Could I scoot down to the branch below? Then the next? Could I stretch that far? Maybe.

Headfirst, I reached with my left paw. My right arm remained hooked on the branch on which I crouched. I stretched. Then stretched a little further. My toe brushed the lower limb. This rung was not sturdy like the one I now desperately clung to. It gave way to my touch. I hung there with indecision, strung out like a rabbit ready for skinning. My arm muscles cried out. If I dangled there any longer, I would become too weak to pull myself back up. I had to commit. Go back? Or…?

I let go.

My feeble toehold on the lower rung slipped. I fell against the next branch below. Scrambling for a lifeline, hind claws extracted, I miraculously grasped the limb. I hugged it tightly until the sound of cracking wood broke the silence and my illusion of safety. My lifeline split from the trunk. Squeezing my eyes shut I clung to the branch. I dropped like a pine cone clamoring against every limb on its way to the ground.

Branch after branch poked and prodded me on my long, harrowing descent. I called out with a defiant roar. And, as if the cat gods had acknowledged my plea, I came to an abrupt halt.

I dared to open my eyes. A prickly bush had snared me and broken my fall. When I attempted to move it dug its thorns into me clawing at my legs, my belly my face, even my nose. I hurt all over. I let out a feeble howl and peered at the ground below. It would be an easy leap. Relief washed over me drowning out my frustration. I was still alive. And even better, I was on my way to finding Petunia.

CHAPTER TWENTY

I pushed through the dense thorns and sized up the pavers below. I had come this far. No more fear. I jumped.

A paralyzing pain shot from my shoulder, down my foreleg, and grasped my paw as I hit the ground. I cried out. Unable to support my body's weight my leg gave way. I collapsed onto my side. Stunned, I lay there trying to figure out what had happened.

I struggled to stand, again. And again, the tormenting pain. I whimpered and attempted to shake off the disabling throbs in my shoulder. Once more I nearly toppled over. I tried a different tack. I lifted my offending paw. The pain eased. I took a faltering step, then another. Limping on, hopping, and stumbling, I headed for the river. I would follow the waterway until I reached the highway that runs through town.

My going was slow. I had only made it halfway to the river road when the relentless needling in my shoulder forced me to stop and catch my breath. Sitting down, I reached back to lick at my troublesome shoulder, but the effort made the pain worse. Worry and disappointment crept over me, infecting my determination. Now *all* my joints ached. What if the scary confusion sets in? Nearly blinded by the pain somehow, I pushed on.

A muffled whisper of a mew too close for comfort sent my hair on end. Arching my back, I leaped into the air and spun around. Landing big and bad, ready to face the predator, my leg screamed with a vengeance. Or was it me? Fear and anguish blinded me. Bracing for the worst I screeched.

Another cottony murmur of a mew rang with familiarity and brought me to my senses. I blinked. It was only Wild Girl. Why was I surprised? She had a way of appearing out of nowhere. She padded up to me. Closer than ever before. Purring loudly, she rubbed her cheek against mine.

Feeling foolish I forgot about my aching shoulder and purred back. Always perplexed by my reactions to Wild Girl, confusion clouded around me. Not now! I shook it off and took a couple of faltering steps. The unsettling bewilderment cleared. Of course, I was headed for the river. I may get a little disorientated, but I will never forget my quest. Petunia was waiting for me. Who else could make me so determined to abandon my cushy life with Mom?

Already tired, I blamed it on the pain racking through my body. Still, I pressed on. Wild Girl's footfall padded softly behind me. I found it comforting that she was going to accompany me. But she was young. Soon she would tire of me and my frailties.

As I plodded along, various night sounds caught my attention. The loudest was the silence. Then, a faint rustling, of what I didn't know, followed by a hooting owl and a graceful splash of a steelhead trout in the river. Then, like an assassin's bullet, the resonating screech of a raptor pierced the darkness sending chills up my spine. I ducked for cover and remained until I realized it was only an echo from across the river. I sent my gratitude to the cat gods,

I made it to the edge of the road. Sound travels a long way on a still night. Taking on a pensive attitude, I sat down and scanned the area.

No longer holding back, Wild Girl came up beside me as a truck's engine hummed in the distance. The bend in the road reached into the blackness. The big rig's engine grew louder as its headlights cast ghostly shadows in the trees. Growing louder its roar busted through the darkness, exploded into sight, and thundered past. In a blink, the logger truck vanished around the next turn, and the deceiving calm returned. Taking a deep breath, I swayed back and forth, preparing to make my dash.

But I waited, not sure if I heard more traffic sounds. Roads are dangerous. Mom often pointed out the misfortunate creatures along the highways who didn't make it across. Bracing for the pain, I sprinted across the road. Keening from the fire in my shudder I stumbled midway and fell flat on my chin. My heart accelerated into double time not from the effort but from the fear of an oncoming vehicle.

Wild Girl appeared at my side. Just her presence cheered me on. In agony, I scrambled to get up only to collapse again. The sound of an oncoming car spurred me to reach past the hurt. I stood on shaky legs. With a clumsy gait, I lumbered to the other side just as the car swooshed by. No sooner had I exhaled in relief than I gasped in panic. Wild Girl! Where was she? I spun around, dreading finding her as roadkill.

"Mew."

I leaped in the air. Spinning around I came face to face with her. Happy relief shot through me. But it was short-lived. Anger rushed in to hide the foolishness I felt. I dropped my tail, pinned my ears back, and growled. Wild Girl just smiled at me.

Like a heavy coat on a hot day, a weariness came over me and weighed me down. My good legs buckled as if made of lead. Bone weary, all I wanted to do was go home.

Wild Girl rubbed up against me and chirped. Trotting toward the river she twitched her tail, then raised it like a flag. Her way of saying "Follow me." Steeling myself against the pain and exhaustion I inhaled a deep breath and followed.

She disappeared into a thicket of shrubbery nestled on the river's edge. At her heels, I nudged into the thick vegetation. At least there were no thorns. I found myself in the middle of the leafy cave. Wild Girl nodded toward a soft bed of river grasses that she had hollowed into a bed. She was inviting me to make myself comfortable.

It wasn't my tiger bed, but the matted bed of grass never looked so good. I hobbled over and collapsed. My eyes drooped in exhaustion, and I quickly faded off into a restless sleep.

I was drifting out to sea. I called out to Mom who was crying on the beach. I paddled fervently trying to reach her on the shore, but I only drifted further away.

Among the choppy waves, a log tossed and churned. I swam toward it and as I climbed on, it transformed into Petunia. Carrying me she swam easily back to shore. Feeling safe and warm, my heart swelled with love. But when we reached the shoreline, she evaporated into the sand and Mom was gone. I was alone again.

I woke up whimpering. Wild Girl lifted her head and chirped, "It's okay." She didn't know what I had dreamed, but I still felt foolish. Standing, I stretched hoping to work out the unnerving ache in my leg which had become a slow but tolerable searing sensation. Dawn lit the eastern mountain ridge turning the sky powdery gray. Thirst and hunger pangs reminded me of my awaiting food and water dishes at home.

I glanced at Wild Girl. She must have read my mind. Approaching me she pawed at something lying at the edge of the grassy nest. It smelled of tuna. I sniffed it. Was it tuna? My stomach growled a yes. I licked it. Not bad. I took a nibble, then bit off a small chunk. My mouth watered in anticipation, and I chomped it down. The morsel tasted fresh and cold from the river, like no Fancy Feast I'd ever eaten. Ripping off another hunk, I barely chewed it before swallowing. I was hungrier than I thought.

After gorging down several mouthfuls, I remembered Wild Girl and paused. Stepping away I nodded at the meal at my feet. Acknowledging with that dainty chirp of hers she stepped up to the meal. True to her unimposing manner, she nibbled a small chunk at a time as she was dining with royalty.

After dinner, we both washed up as the new day crept up over the pines and sprinkled the river with sparkles. Completing our duties, my belly full I resumed my trek. As I headed downstream, I glanced back. Wild Girl remained where I had left her. She was not going any farther. Probably best that she didn't. She would only be in the way when I found Petunia.

CHAPTER TWENTY-ONE

The numbness made me think my leg and shoulder were better. But after I had gone a little further, lightheadedness caused me to swerve and stray from the animal trial I followed. The trees danced and the water swirled around me reminding me of the time when Mom took me for a ride on the Missoula Carousel in Montana. The music and the ride were so much fun. But this was not. There was no music. My stomach churned. I lay down at the edge of the path and tried to hug the earth. I thought I might... Ugh! I retched.

When the dizziness and the miserable roiling eased, I stood on wobbly legs. Taking a few test steps, then a few more, I continued without the merry-go-round effect... until blackness engulfed me.

How much time had passed before the darkness receded, I don't know, but when it did, I found myself perched in a nearby tree while the world carried on around me. Birds chirped. The river slid, smooth as glass on its way to the ocean. I felt peaceful… until I noticed my still body lying on the path below. My head rested on my paws as if I were taking a nap. And yet, here I sat high above in a tree watching life go by. How? When had I climbed this tree? My pain was gone.

I could see everywhere. Wild Girl sat at the edge of the road, her tail twitching looking back and forth as she checked for traffic. Satisfied the coast was clear, she made one last swish of her tail, scampered across, and ran up the hill to the house.

It was not like her leaving me so vulnerable sleeping on the path like this. She didn't look back as she scaled the patio steps and took a position at the slider door. She didn't use her gentle voice but instead, she wailed. Her bawling carried to the river where I lay. What was she doing? Trying to take my place? Was she ratting on me? Telling Mom, I was leaving her? But that was unlike Wild Girl either. But leaving me alone and vulnerable? I wanted to get up, run and hide. Yet, from my perch in the tree, I still lay on the path sleeping.

Mom's crying woke me. She stood over me where I lay on the path. I looked up at her. Her face contorted in worry as she hammered out her questions. "What happened to you? I've been looking all night for you! What're you doing way out here all by yourself?" She swiped her arm across her tear-streaked face. Without waiting for me to answer she knelt beside me. She jostled me even though I could tell she tried to pick me up as gently as she could. The intense throbbing in my shoulder returned with a fiery vengeance and racked my body. Unable to bear it, I cried out with a feeble meow before, once again, the blackness overtook me.

The next thing I knew, once again, I found myself looking down from my perch in the tree. Wild Girl remained crouched on the sidelines as Mom scooped me up and ran, down the path, across the road, and back to the house.

She didn't take me inside but instead, yanked open the car door and laid me on the passenger seat. With trembling hands, she covered me with her Harley Davidson sweatshirt she kept in the car for emergencies. She tucked it around me. "Always be prepared," she used to tell me. "You never know when you might be caught out in the cold." I realized I was shaking, too.

She dashed into the house, grabbed her purse and keys, and clambered down the stairs. The car tires spat gravel as she backed out onto the street, then floored it when she hit the river road.

Mom kept swiping at her tears the whole way into town until she pulled into the veterinary clinic. What? I was not in the mood. I did *not* want to go there!

I knew I could stay with my body. Or give up. Leave it behind. The choice was mine to make. But if I decided to give up somehow, I knew I couldn't change my mind, there would be no turning back. But would that be so bad? I would have no more pain.

I decided to wait. For now. Inside a young girl with blonde streaks in her hair and wearing a smock decorated with playful kittens escorted Mom and me into an exam room. Taking me from Mom's arms, Blondie laid me on the cold steel table. Mom hovered over me, petting me with a shaky hand as her cooing words tumbled out on her sobs.

Blondie, who had turned her back to me, now approached, her arm poised in the air as she grasped a… what… a syringe? A clamor of alarms sounded off in my head. She was part of the Peoples Humane Army! I tried to bolt. But she was quick to pin me down. I should have just given up. Now they were going to kill me. The stories were true. That's what happens if you try to run away. I felt the prick of the needle and cold serum flooded through my body.

And the blackness returned.

* * * * * *

Low voices lulled me awake. "Hello, Sportster." Blondie, who had stuck me with the needle a moment ago now smiled down at me. "We're so glad you came back to us. How are you feeling?" Her finger caressed the top of my head. Where's her needle? She probably had it hidden behind her back.

How do I feel?! I let out a choke of a meow. You try to kill me and then make all nicey-nice and ask how I feel? I looked around. What had they done with my mom? My tongue stuck to the roof of my mouth and my head felt as if someone had stuffed it full of cotton balls. Whatever they had done with Mom, I was probably next. I had to get out of there. I tried to stand but a blanket of weakness weighed me down.

I glanced at my front leg through blurry eyes. It appeared to be wrapped in cotton, and yet it felt as if a boulder rested on it. The rest of me seemed to be floating on a cloud. A spurt of adrenaline shot through me in an attempt to jump-start my body, but it died quickly leaving me content to succumb to whatever was going on. A whimper escaped before I closed my eyes and rested my head in defeat.

"No. No, Sportster. Don't go back to sleep. Let's get some fluids down you. I know you're thirsty." It wasn't a needle she had in her hand, but it was similar. She lifted my head and poked it in my mouth. Cool water flooded over my tongue. I swallowed and then sucked on it. I couldn't remember anything tasting so good. I gazed up at her with an apology in my eyes.

She broke out with a big smile. "You're welcome, little man." She shoved another eyedropper in my mouth, and I sucked it dry. "Later we'll give you some ooey-gooey food and if you eat it then we'll let you go home."

Home? The thought cheered me on. After I took a couple more

drinks Blondie picked me up and set me in a cage stuffed with warm blankets. I nuzzled into them.

"Nice huh? Fresh out of the dryer." She set a water bowl and a dish of some kind of tuna-smelling mush in front of me, but I paid it no mind. My eyelids drooped. "You need to rest. I'll come back and check on you later."

In my foggy state, murmuring voices faded in and out and then floated away like the wake of the fishing boats slushing against the shore. I dozed, dreaming of romping in grassy meadows and along gurgling rivers with Petunia, Wild Girl, and Mom like one big happy family.

When I woke long afternoon shadows stretched across the linoleum floor. The clinic's hustle and bustle had quieted when Blondie came back to check on me, I sat upright, awake, and clear-headed.

"Hello, Sportster. How ya doing?" She scratched some notes on her clipboard.

Bum leg and all, I stood.

"Look at you! You'll figure out how to maneuver around soon enough." She focused on my food bowl. Only the mashed ingredients along the bottom edges of the dish remained. That made her happy.

"Good job. And you're looking bright-eyed and ready to meet the world. Let's call your mom and tell her you want to go home." Marking on her clipboard, she spun around and disappeared down the hall.

❁ ❁ ❁ ❁ ❁

Mom thanked Blondie and paid the bill. As she hurried to the car, she held up my carrier at eye level and peered in. Her brow furrowed with serious wrinkles. She chattered non-stop all the way home. "When I discovered you were gone the neighbors teamed up with me to search for you. I imagined finding your body, mangled by some coyote or eagle. or stomped on by a mama deer" She glanced over at me. "Is that what happened to you? How did you end up all by yourself at the river with a dislocated shoulder?" She paused a moment and caught her breath. "We searched until it was just too dark to go on. By morning I was so distraught!" Tears leaked down her cheek, but then she shot me a big smile. "But you're going to be okay. "She stuck her finger through the carrier door's grate, and I rubbed up against it as she scratched the top of my head. "You owe Wild Girl big time. Do you know that? The girl was relentless. She showed up this morning at the patio door meowing and meowing."

Mom went on to explain that every time she came out to see what Wild Girl's problem was, the cat would run away, then stop, and look back at her. At first, Mom figured the cat ran away because she was wild. "Anyway, like I said Wild Girl didn't give up. Finally, I figured out that she was trying to get me to follow her. When I saw you lying there on the path, I thought you were dead."

Mom eased the car into the carport. "We're home." Once inside, she helped me from the carrier and laid me in my tiger bed near my food and water. Content to be home, I took a long breath and relaxed.

But with my next breath, Petunia's image popped into my mind. I moaned, but not from the pain. How would I ever find her now?

CHAPTER TWENTY-TWO

Although my shoulder muscles protested, I hobbled to the litterbox. No chore came easy these days. After I finished my business, I made a sloppy attempt to cover it. Unable to do the chore without falling over, I slinked away.

In the kitchen, I stared up at the faucet and howled. Quick to respond, Mom trotted up behind me and lifted me onto the counter. After turning on the water, she waited while I drank my fill. I hated that she watched every move. But I hated even more that I needed her to be there for me.

Before she lowered me to the floor, she wrapped me in a big hug and held me close. Before I could resist, she shoved a syringe in my mouth and squirted a paste onto my tongue. Hmmm? Peanut butter. Pretty tasty. She waited, making sure I swallowed, then giving me a quick kiss on the head, she set me down on the floor. "There! That will help with your pain."

I clumped into the living room and flopped my butt in my tiger bed which Mom had placed in the pool of sunshine streaming from the long window. Still, she hovered over me.

"You soak up some sunshine." She studied me for a moment. Assured I was comfortable she retreated to her office. But before she disappeared down the hall, she called over her shoulder. "I'll check on you in a bit."

Once she was out of sight I sat up. I wanted to wash my face and scratch my itching leg without toppling over. I hated this helplessness. The anger that Mom was doing this to me grew. How am I going to do anything let alone find Petunia? I stood up and made a half-assed attempt to shake off the suffocating cloud of darkness which followed me everywhere ever since she started feeding me the peanut butter. Teetering, I fell over. Growling, I remained where I lay dejected and alone refusing to cry out for help.

An ugly crow swooped past the window and then making a U-turn, flew back. Flapping his wings he hovered there, his beady eyes homing in on me as I lay helpless. He called me out with sinister caws and began hammering at the pane with his beak. The rat-a-tat of the staccato pecking and his n evil laugh crept up my spine Needles of frustration and anguish pricked under my skin until I couldn't take it anymore. He wouldn't stop.

Like a caged lion, I lashed out at the cast where it dug into my armpit. To my surprise, a big hunk of the plaster gave way. A tinge of hope pushed through my clouded brain and spurred me on. I attacked the cumbersome sleeve. Ripping and tearing to the cadence of the jeering heckles from the evil-eyed bird, I flung the chunks of plaster into the air. With each bite, my power returned until I became strong with the vengeance of a crazed cat.

When the last hunk of plaster crumbled to the floor, I was free. I tested my bum leg. Standing I took a couple of steps. I wavered with an awkward stiffness but braved a couple more. No pain. I was good to go. I was so done with everything. This house. Mom, The birds. If I hurried, I could make it to the highway by dark. I tiptoed down the hall past Mom, clacking away on her laptop, and slipped into the bedroom closet.

My first attempt to jump onto the dresser brought me crashing to the floor. A wave of dizziness swept over me, and I sat down. I just needed a minute. Without the albatross wrapped around my leg, I began the soothing ritual of licking my paws and washing my face…

Until Mom appeared at the closet entrance her face wrinkled with worry. "What's going on? Did you fall? "But only seconds passed before the lines of worry deepened into an angry frown. "What have you done?" Kneeling, she scooped me up, held me in the air, and inspected my now unencumbered foreleg.

The concern in her voice cut me more than her scolding words.

"Now you've done it. This will not do. Now, you've got to go back to the vet."

I hung my head. Outside the crows cawed with delight.

No cooing sweet nothings, no kisses. Mom had snapped. It was over. Mom packed me into my carrier. She headed down the river road. To the veterinarian.

Mom dropped me off at the reception front desk. She didn't even go in with me. So, she was mad? I was too. I just want to find my Petunia. How could I explain? As Blondie delivered me into the bedlam of barking and meowing, I let out a caterwaul that shook the walls of my carrier.

Blondie approached the doctor, but he waved her off. He didn't want to see me either. Blondie dragged me from my cage and proceeded to slap the now familiar gooey, offensive-smelling plaster all over my leg again. Didn't they know I would just rip it off again? I was so done with everyone's treatment of me. As if she read my thoughts, Blondie whipped out a contraption like a rabbit from a magician's hat. Shoving it over my head she tied it so tight around my neck I coughed. I screamed out a spineless threat. Blondie didn't know I had no backup. No matter if Mom was no longer on my side of the fence, I was ready to go down biting and clawing. Wait 'til my mom sees this! She will not stand for it! I hissed and growled, but Blondie just shoved me back into my carrier as if to let me stew.

Mom was not her chatty self on the ride home. That was okay. I was not talking to her either. Back at home, she opened the carrier to release me. I tried to bolt out the door but now, not only did the cast deter me, but the damned cone prevented me from demonstrating my indignation. I whimpered.

Mom's demeanor softened. My mood lightened with hope as she fiddled and shoved until my head and the annoying contraption squeezed through the carrier's opening. But she made no moves to rid me of it. Why was she doing this to me? Didn't she care anymore? I crawled over to my tiger bed, turned my back to her, and plopped down.

I sulked. Petunia… or her ghost… waited for me. I couldn't separate the two ideas anymore. I didn't want to go on without her, especially now I t was like she'd lit a fire inside me. It was becoming obvious Mom was done with me, so there was no place for me here anymore. I batted at a dust bunny rolling past. I would escape again. But for now, I had no choice but to surrender to the situation. I would find a way to be rid of my restraints. Mom certainly had no intention of removing them. I would wait.

CHAPTER TWENTY-THREE

While I waited, doubts that I would ever be free again swarmed like flies over roadkill. I swatted at another dust bunny, but it attached itself to my plastered leg.

Wild Girl peered through the panes of the French doors as she did every morning. I think she worried about me. At least she cared. As was her habit she moved to the pond and took up her ritual of preening. Of all the wild cats I encountered during my travels, and there were many in the campgrounds, not one ever wore a cast or an unyielding albatross like mine.

Sensing me staring she looked back at me. Her mouth opened slightly. A mew I couldn't hear escaped followed by one of her sultry blinks. To my surprise, she wasn't laughing at me. She was waiting, too. I sighed and hobbled to my litter box. Did she feel sorry for me? Probably. I know I did.

After finishing my business, which was not an easy chore in my condition, I returned to my tiger bed. Wild Girl sat fixated on the pond's waterfall, probably contemplating her day and what to explore in her vast domain. After her meditation, she would saunter down to the meadow on the lower level of the property. There she would bask in the sunshine until afternoon until the heat drove her to move. From there she sought out shade under the fruit trees by the creek. The fruit grove blocked my view, but I knew the riverbank was her territory too.

I closed my eyes. The sultry aroma from her bed of grasses she had shared with me that first night came to mind. A heated flush stirred my numbed senses. My mouth went dry. Licking my lips, I could still taste the fresh fish she had fed me.

My brain yanked me back to the present. *Are you really going to leave again when you get the chance.?* A cry escaped as if my heart was not happy with my intentions. I tried to explain it. "I'm going to come back. I will bring Petunia back with me."

My heart pounded out a fearful beat and my chest tightened. *"What if Mom doesn't want another cat?"*

"Don't worry, Mom will love Petunia too. You'll see. Hadn't she taken me in? She'll see how much Petunia means to me." Even I didn't buy that argument. I'd bite her. I'd tried to run away. Mom was probably done with me anyway.

But my brain wanted to hammer the point home. *"Remember those helpless cute kittens someone left in a box on her doorstep? She didn't want them. And they were cute. She gave every one of them away."*

"That's because I *made* it clear *I* didn't want them. I can make it just as clear that I want Petunia to stay."

An involuntary harrumph of disapproval.

"I know. You're worried about Mom," I argued. "But she'll be okay." I tried to dismiss the doubts clamoring in my head. I stood up to change positions but when I tried to turn around, the cone caught the edge of my tiger bed, and I plopped back down. I growled.

A stabbing hurt jabbed at my gut. *"Do you really believe she'll be ok?"* The haunting voice would not let up.

"Why don't you just shut up?" The force of my retort startled me. I pinned back my ears and growled.

Again, the tightness stabbed my tummy. *"I could shut up, but that won't change anything."*

The annoying voice was right. Who was I kidding? Mom depended on me. She had no one else. She had *him* those couple of times when he came to visit, but he didn't stay. If he had, maybe she would not need me like she does.

But he didn't stay, so now she needs you.

"But I'm going to come back!"

"What if she's so mad and hurt she doesn't want you back? Have you thought of that? She's already upset with you big time?"

Outside, Wild Girl glanced in my direction. Could she hear me arguing with no one? She didn't sneer. Meeting her stare, I muttered out loud. "I'll bet all the Fancy Feast in the world you never had to be a cone-head or hobble around on a peg leg." But of course, she couldn't hear me.

The voice again. *"Do I have to remind you? Wild Girl's life is no fairy tale. I know you've heard her crying to come in when it's raining and cold."*

"But she doesn't want to *stay* inside!" I wanted to scream. "She won't even let Mom pick her up! She's free. She's not going to give that up. No shots, no peg legs, no cones for her! She catches her dinners fresh from the river and drinks crispy cold water whenever she wants."

"Who are you trying to convince?"

I hissed and spat into the air. "You! You're the one all hung up on Mom. Have *you* forgotten how you feel about Petunia!?" I flushed again. I was arguing with a voice that no one else heard. I gasped as another piercing pain that the peanut butter paste couldn't quell clenched my stomach t like a vise.

Then silence.

I hung my cone-head. If it was my conscience giving me a hard time, I didn't need anyone arguing Mom's case. I knew the stakes if I left Mom to search for Petunia. Mom and I had been together since I was a kitten chasing my tail. But if only I could explain my side.

* * * * * *

I was only six months old when Mom took me in. Stuck with strangers, I worried that my real mom was angry that I left. And at night I lay awake wondering whether Petunia was dead or alive.

I was only six months old and easily distracted. The puffs of fur, like Styrofoam peanuts from a packing box, floated from the grooming tables and danced to the floor. I'd twirl and pounce, and swat them, sending the furry clouds into the air while my new mom and the other groomers cheered me on.

I was six months old and really missing my real mom, my siblings, and Petunia. Their haunting mews came to me in my sleep. We miss you, too. Please come back. Find us. And I would answer. "Not now. Wait 'til morning," I promised with the good intentions of my kitten heart. "In the morning, I'll go back. I'll look for you and I'll find you."

But other voices heavy with fear added their opinions and drowned out my innocent intentions. *"You can't go! What will become of you? What about the wild dogs prowling the streets? What if Petunia doesn't want you? Your family didn't? After all, no one has come looking for you."*

Only six months old, I questioned my good intentions. How preposterous to think Petunia might want a kitten like me. Especially after I failed to keep her safe from the big Rottweiler.

So, the promised day never came for my loved ones or for Petunia. I never found the courage to go back. Instead, the shame came and like a pickpocket, it robbed me of any joy I gained from my new life with Mom.

Like a prisoner, I lay in my tiger bed and began to recount the hundreds of moments over the years I'd shared with Mom. Dancing with her. Purring and snuggling to comfort her when she cried over her lost love. Walking in the forest, along the riverbank, and just watching the sunset. Life with Mom has been full. But they were stolen moments that would have belonged to Petunia… if I had returned for her.

Suddenly I was riled. Why should I have to argue my case? I spat into the empty air like a fire-breathing dragon. Not so sure of itself, my heart skipped a beat. Good. I didn't like being pushed into a corner.

I challenged it. "Why so quiet?" I swatted my tail back and forth like a whip. "Let's talk about Petunia. Have you forgotten how you feel about her," I growled out loud. "Have you?"

My heart's hard-core yearning grabbed me, pushing the air from my lungs. But I braced for it. "I didn't think so." My eyes turned to slits. I pinned back my ears. and sucked back the stolen air through tightened lips. My tail was whipping back and forth and back and forth.

I had not wanted to bring up the sweet memories of Petunia. God knows, I've relived them, pined over them, and fell asleep dreaming of them a million times through the years. But I was mad. I pushed back. "I know you remember Petunia. What it was like with her. Her unending patience as she taught me the ways of a wild cat. How she kept me safe. Do you think I'm not aware of all the nights… even last night… when you wait until I sleep?"

My tail beat like a war drum, thump, thump-thump, thump against the hardwood floor. "You think I don't know how you wait until I'm sleeping and sneak in through my mind's back door? And you start rolling the scenes of Petunia and me? Romping in the meadow through the tall grass. Chasing falling leaves whisked by the wind. Pouncing and catching them. How we shared our meals at sunset."

I whimpered knowing the longing and regret which followed my tirade.

"You think I don't suffer the guilt of never going back for her? Never searching for her? I should have hunted until I found her or died trying. I've lived with that regret every day. You never stop with the visions of her. They ravage me like a raptor tearing out my heart."

I bolted up. Damn it! Arching my back, I spiked my fur and howled out loud. "It's your fault! You're the one who has kept her memory alive! All these years! If not for you, we would not be having this argument. "I gasped for a snatch of air. "If not for you, Petunia would only be in a faint mood, a teasing inkling, a passing fancy! I could have forgotten about her. And if not for you, I would not be considering abandoning Mom."

Still no response.

I slumped with the hopelessness of it all. The cone's hard plastic dug against my neck. Like my life, my options were bleak. I lose Mom. Or I lose Petunia. Maybe both. No matter how I play it, I'll be the loser. But I've been the loser since I was a kitten.

My bones ached. I sucked in a deep breath. I've put off this quest for far too long. I don't want to. I *won't* leave this earth without making things right. I know there are no guarantees with Petunia. She may only be a ghost. But if she isn't. And if I really do love her. I don't want her living out the rest of her life thinking I abandoned her. No one needs to think they're not wanted. I know how it feels.

It's time. If I put it off any longer, I *will* be too old. No matter the plastered leg. Nor the cone. And if Mom still loves me, she'll understand. I've activated lion mode before. Now it's time to activate love mode.

CHAPTER TWENTY-FOUR

Beaded droplets from the waterfall shimmered on the Calle Lilies' wimpled heads. What lurked in the dark pond water beneath no longer worried me. The possibility of finding Petunia left me wanting to chase my tail and play hide-and-seek. Nothing was as bad as it seemed yesterday.

I twisted around to groom myself and calm the excitement building inside me. My tongue met sterile plastic. I growled and sank back into my plush tiger bed. I took deep breaths instead. Inhaling the cone contraption's manufactured chemical scent, I sneezed. But it was okay. I'd come to terms with my limited situation. I may be a cone-headed clunker with a plaster leg, eating processed food, and watching the laughing birds fly. But it's only for now. Soon enough I will go out and find Petunia. The excitement cemented my determination. I had made the decision. There was no turning back.

. I memorized Mom's every habit. She had a routine. She was a careful person. I could count on one paw the times she accidentally left a door open or unlatched... and fewer times that I had been alert enough to notice.

But those times when I slipped out unnoticed? Oh boy! I was

pumped with the thrill of adventure like I am now. Once, I enjoyed an entire hour exploring to my liking before Mom discovered my escape. I purred remembering the freedom. For that one hour, I was a top cat, and there was no feeling like it.

But for now, I plotted my escape. Waiting for the right time. Mom trusted me. She often stands on the deck, the door ajar, and calls out a good morning to neighbor, Gil who walks his dog to the river every morning. I made mental notes and schemed.

Before Petunia appeared on the computer screen, I had not cared much about going outside. I am easily tired these days. On our walks, I rarely insisted on sniffing every rock and leaf, nor do I investigate every bush and tree trunk. I do enjoy lying on the cool grass, chasing a bug now and then. And once in a while, I'll spring up to swat at a blackbird or Jay. They like to swoop down cawing out threats to peck out my eyes if I come too close to their chicks.

I have become laid back in my later years. I blame Mom. Or is it my fault she caters to me? I know how to hound her with pathetic mews and penetrating stares to score treats and fresh water from the faucet. All I have to do is shiver and Mom moves my tiger bed over the floor register. Sometimes when my bones ache, and I hesitate to jump onto her lap, she lifts me. On rare occasions, I wake from a nap and find my bed wet, but she never scolds me. Today was not one of those rare times. Standing up on achy legs, I teetered and hurried down the hall to the mud room.

But after several steps, I balked. I found myself where? Not in the mud room. I studied my surroundings. The linoleum floor was white not this darker gray. Where was my litter box? I didn't recognize the throw rug. The room reminded me of Mom's bathroom… but it wasn't. Was I dreaming? I blinked. No. An icy panic grabbed me. How could I be lost? In my own house? I needed Mom. bellowed out a howl that could be heard at the riverbank. She always comes when I call. I hollered out again.

Where is she? My catnip stuffed mouse donning its tiny Harley

Davidson denim jacket lay in the corner. I knew it was mine. But knowing it didn't make me feel better.

At the other end of the house, a door clicked open and slammed shut. The sound of Mom's familiar footfall t came closer and closer. I recognized her scent before she rounded the corner.

Her voice, higher than usual, indicated a mother's concern. "What's wrong little buddy?"

Cooing and clucking she knelt, swept me up, and pressed me close to her breast. Breathing in her familiar scent, I melted. My head cleared. I had wandered into our spare bathroom. We rarely go in there. No wonder I was confused. I nuzzled her arm, and she bent down and kissed me.

"Did you get lost again?"

No, I was not lost. Compared to our life in the motorhome our new house was so big.

"I was outside. But I'm here now." She hugged me tightly and kissed me again and again.

No need to make such a big fuss. I squirmed and twisted loose from her dramatic grasp.

Mom cried out. "Oh no!" With a clonk and a thud, I landed on my side and then scrambled to stand.

"Oh, you poor baby!" She lifted me to a standing position. "Don't worry. You're ok. And tomorrow we go to the vet."

The vet?! What kind of torture was she dreaming up now? Hell no!

When her phone buzzed from her office, she gathered me in her arms and hurried to her desk. Sitting down, she positioned me on her lap, read the notification icon, and smiled.

CHAPTER TWENTY-FIVE

Mom tapped the icon on her phone. "It's Carol." Carol's face bursting with excitement radiated from the laptop. She reminded me of a cat ready to pounce.

Mom grinned at her friend. "Hi, girlfriend. What's hap—?"

"The ranch sold!"

"Super! I am so excited for you." Mom tensed with the excitement of her friend's news.

But my stomach flip-flopped. The string of hope I had been batting around about seeing Petunia tangled into a knot and died like a dead daddy long-legs. How would I find Petunia now if she moved?

Carol leaned away from the camera's eye and then bobbed back into view dangling a set of keys in front of her face.

"The keys to your new home?" Mom leaned closer to the computer screen. "You've already found a new place?" Feeding her friend's gaiety Mom scooted to the edge of her chair.

Carol laughed out loud. "Sort of." Her chair creaked as she jostled up and down. I thought she might fall out of it. She dropped the keys on her desk, and after rustling some papers, she held up a photo in front of the camera's lens. A motorhome filled Mom's screen.

"You bought an RV?" I felt Mom's excitement increase. Mom loved people who had RVs.

"Yes!" Carol set the photo aside. "I'm so excited. What do you think?" She didn't wait for Mom to answer. She drew Petunia into the camera's view. "Petunia loves it!"

My heart skipped a beat, then exploded like a racehorse bursting from the starting gate. The possibility of being free of any confusion and aches, the cone, my plastered leg… all vanished. I was six months old again.

Scarlett, who I am certain is Petunia, sniffed the laptop's camera. Her bright pink nose and her adorable black smudge filled Mom's screen. My heart was off and running.

Mom sat at attention. "Wow! Really, an RV? Have you planned your first trip? It's beautiful. Sportster and I had planned on surprising you and Scarlett by showing up on your doorstep. I was going to help you pack. But Sportster had a mishap, and we couldn't go."

"Oh no. What happened? Is he ok?"

Mom smiled. "He's fine. He's recovering."

Before I could protest, Mom pulled me from her lap and held me up in the air showing me off like a prize steelhead she'd caught from the river. I hung in front of Petunia for her and the entire world to see. My cone-head bobbled, and my plastered leg dangled like a piece of meat at a slaughterhouse. I stuttered out a prayer begging that Scarlett… or Petunia… whoever she was… was only a ghost.

Petunia howled. I shivered. Indignity and anger flushed through me. I screamed like a cornered cat and sank my teeth into Mom's arm. Twisting from her grasp, I thudded onto the floor.

"Ow! Sportster! You bit me!" Mom bent down to catch me, but the cat gods had finally taken pity on my mortifying humiliation and allowed me to scramble to my feet. I ran, clunk-clunk, clunk-clunk, out of the room, down the hall, and under the bed. I was never coming out.

I wanted to cry. I wanted to kill something. I couldn't believe Mom had reduced me to a spectacle for her amusement. What was wrong with her? Even Petunia screamed with laughter. Or was she horrified too? I shivered again with contempt.

And I still had to face the vet tomorrow. Whatever demeaning thing they might be plotting against me next frightened me. What was happening? I gazed up at the heavens, but my head struck the sharp metal frame. "Okay. Really?"

If the Gods were daring me, I would take the challenge. I would jump from the closet window again if it were not for the choking cone digging into my neck. I moaned, then burped. Burning acid bubbled from my throat. I heaved. Yellow bile spewed onto the floor and soaked my plastered leg. I retched again. As if the bed had collapsed and was crushing me, my last bit of spirit turned to dust. I stared at my plastered paw, now yellowed with bile. I was NOT going to clean it off.

Mom's demoralizing cackles crept under the bed and found me. Like the claws of an angry she-cat, they cut through me. I thought I heard Petunia's delicate sniggering, too. They were having a hell of a party at my expense. I had become a clown, the jester of the house. How could I be such a fool as to think I might find my spot in heaven, a place in the sun? I curled into a tight ball and squeezed my eyes shut.

❊ ❊ ❊ ❊ ❊ ❊

I slept in a field of flowers, my chin on my paws. A cool breeze tickled my fur. Flicking my ear, I shook my head at the annoyance but didn't wake. A soft, sultry meow much like Petunia's intruded on my dreamy thoughts. Pausing from my musings yet still in slumber, I raised my head. I couldn't squeeze my heart shut fast enough. It swelled with hope. Was it Petunia? Dare I look?

In my dream, I tensed. My heart had slipped onto the scene and attempted to cheer me on. *"Of course! Look!"*

But I didn't. I knew better even though it was only a dream. If I turned to look, I would shatter.

But temptation taunted me. *"Not just one more time?"*

Like in a sci-fi movie, Dad materialized. He stretched out beside me, his hooked tail lolling in the tall grass while he gazed toward the horizon. He didn't say anything, but I knew he believed in impossible dreams coming true. I shrugged off his presence and turned my back and said, *"Fool me once, shame on you. Fool me twice, shame on me."* But I couldn't help feeling his presence was like coming home, although I told myself *"It's only a dream."* A bell tolled in the dreamy fog.

In the morning, the noise from Mom's rustling as she primped in front of the mirror woke me. I used to enjoy watching her prepare for the day ahead while I performed my grooming rituals. I missed that. I peeked out from under the bed.

With my mind distracted by pleasantries, the memory of yesterday's catastrophe charged in like a bully and took over. I groaned and my stomach cramped. Yesterday's laughter strutted around, bragging of its victory. Any shred of pride I might have been clinging to shriveled up like a nut in the summer heat.

I tried to move. The stiffness from sleeping all night on the hard floor discouraged me. It was okay. I didn't want to get up. I didn't want to eat either. I sniffed the stale air under the bed. At least I hadn't wet myself. Today Mom was taking me to the vet again. I couldn't imagine what kind of torture they would dream up next. And then my heart sank. I knew.

CHAPTER TWENTY-SIX

As Mom drove toward town, I no longer had to imagine what kind of torture I would be facing. I knew. I was almost relieved.

This was the *no-return trip* to the vet. Wasn't it? You know, the one you never come home from? But I didn't care. Death could not be worse than what I've already gone through. I had only wanted to see Petunia for real, one last time, to make amends to her and hope by chance she could forgive me and want me back. But now that was not going to happen.

Yesterday's circus in which Mom was the ringleader had finished me off. She had crushed the last kibble of pride and the last shred of dignity that I had clung to so perilously. The thin threads of self-respect which allowed me to barely hold my head up were gone. Any hope someone might see me as more than a throwaway cat, vanished. Dad's guttural voice came to me. "You can't change the spots on a leopard." He was right. A throwaway cat is all I've ever been.

The tires thumped down the river road as if a rock were lodged in the tread. The car swayed at every curve, aggravating the grinding ache in my joints. My tummy roiled.

A guy can withstand nearly anything… hunger from not eating for days, blistered pads, from traveling endless miles, and even the loss of his home's comfort and safety… He can handle it all if the one he loves waits at the end of his journey. He will risk everything to conquer the world and die trying… if he believes it will make a better life for his loved ones.

But Mom had killed that dream. Petunia had cried out in horror when she realized my pathetic condition. So, there would be no use trying to find her. Even if she hadn't, I could never face her again, not even her ghost!

Yesterday's crowing and snorting from Mom and Petunia still rattled in my head as Mom pulled up to the veterinary hospital. This was it. I was ready to end this misery. I really was a throwaway cat. I dropped my heavy cone-head, and it landed like dead weight on my plastered leg. After a lifetime of hiding my vulnerability behind a pompous attitude and pretending I was someone I was not, the stark realization hit me. BAM! Like a mountain lion takes down a deer. I was defenseless. I couldn't pretend anymore.

I was old and pathetic. No one cared. Mom didn't want to keep me around in the condition I was in. The cone and the plastered leg? They just became a couple more nails of desperation and self-pity for the coffin in which I had already buried myself—a casket already lined with guilt from my past failures.

So, I was not surprised Mom when loaded me up for this *no-return trip* to the veterinarian. No one was going to rescue me. No more play-acting that I was some kind of glorious cat that I was not.

Mom shut off the car's engine. "We're here." My breath caught. Something in her tone had shifted. She was happy. I swallowed the painful lump in my throat. With a small voice, I let out a weak mew.

She sagged in response but forced caring a smile as if what? Offering some sort of consolation? Her voice wobbled with sadness. "Oh, don't worry, Baby. I promise this won't hurt, and it will be over soon."

So, this was it. The day of no return. The day I had worried about all my life. and now it was going down. Mom was done with me. I squished into the back corner of my carrier. My pompous attitude dried up like a piece of roadkill on the roadside. There would be no tearful goodbyes, like the scenes in the movies. Tears streaming down our faces. *Please don't throw me away!*

A chorus of sparrows sang their lament outside the car window. Birdsongs I would never hear again. I drew the curtain on the theatrical dream of a life with Petunia. My newfound courage to find her and do the right thing was another posturing that had come too late.

The long-suffering apprehension of facing this day, the haunting fear of being found out I was a fraud, along with every puffed-up pretense that I had spit in someone's face... all of it would be behind me now.

I was ready to face my executioner. I squeezed my eyes shut but there was no need. Darkness had already crept into my spirit. I was done. I had given this life my best shot. If the cat gods wanted to take me, I was ready. I didn't even have the will for a dramatic sigh.

My nose twitched catching the rancid smell of pain and death from others who had come here before me. I wanted to retch but I had nothing left in me. Why hadn't the man who had rescued me so long ago just dumped me at the People's Humane Army in the first place? If he had, no one would have to be bothering with me now. I groaned.

Inside, in the veterinary reception area Mom handed me over to Blondie. Just like I thought. Not even a kiss goodbye. With a perky jaunt, the girl carried me away back to the exam room to do the deed. First, she removed my cone and then proceeded to remove my cast. She rattled on in her animated way talking her nonsense. "Aren't you happy to get all this off? You'll be able to run and play again."

I threw her a sharp look. I couldn't help but hate her. Was this a game to her? Why bother removing all the contraptions? Maybe she didn't want the afterlife to know how she had tortured me. When Blondie finished up, she shoved me back into my carrier.

Just when you think you're ready… when you've already dug the hole, covered it up, and called it quits… life can surprise you.

CHAPTER TWENTY-SEVEN

Blondie turned her back to me. Probably preparing the injection. I scrunched into the back corner of the carrier in an attempt to disappear. Like an angry dog shaking its prey until its neck breaks desperation had ahold of me. I trembled uncontrollably.

And then, someone took my limp paw. It wasn't Blondie. She remained across the room preparing her death potion. And then, the despair let go of me. Me. A feeling of weightlessness made me dizzy. And yet a calmness consumed me while my paws remained rooted to the carrier floor. Was I dead?

Mom's face beamed through the wire grate of my cage. In the background, Blondie's cherubic voice. "There you go Sportster! Your Mom's here to take you home."

And then Mom's nicey-nicey voice like the robin's song at first light lured me back from wherever I had gone. "Hey Little Buddy, are you ready to go home?" Her expression was now angelic, no longer lined with worry. She blew me a kiss through the wire door, and with a bouncing stride, carried me to the car.

Wait! What? I'm alive?! I'm breathing?! The car purred, came to life, and began to roll out of the veterinary parking lot. When Mom steered onto the river road, only then did I dare to howl out loud and sing my praises to the cat gods.

Even Mom joined in, chortling off-key to the music on her playlist. With windows down, music turned up, and' feeling the beat' as she called it, she belted out the lyrics to her favorite songs. There wasn't anything she enjoyed more than singing to me while she drove.

I couldn't believe the total turnaround of events. No peg legs. No cone heads. By the time we pulled into the driveway at home, I found the courage to defy the lie I had been so convinced was true. The ride had *not* been a one-way trip. A wonderment washed over me. I felt like I had licked the glue off a hundred Post-It notes. The world was bright. Even the house had taken on a welcoming air.

Mom chattered excitedly as she opened the carrier door. 'You're home. And your leg is well. No cast and no cone!"

Still stunned by my new future I withheld the urge to burst out. I was a new cat, and it was a strange feeling. Along with the removal of the cone and the cast, the feelings of uselessness and self-pity had miraculously been discarded as well. Full of hope I inhaled a deep, cleansing breath. And then with my lost dignity intact, I strutted out of the carrier.

I plopped down in front of the French doors and immediately began my bathing ritual. First, I worked meticulously on my neglected and now freed leg. And then on to the rest of my body parts, I'd been unable to tend to when wearing the cone. As if she'd been waiting for me, Wild Girl sat primly on the other side of the doors. She meowed a cheerful greeting. She was happy to see me.

When I finished my grooming chore Wild Girl stepped up close to the windowpane. Placing her paw on the glass like she had done the first day we'd met, she mewed. This time I felt all warm inside by her gesture. I reached out, and closing my eyes, I did the same. I did not hiss or growl. I didn't have to be the tough guy anymore.

When I opened my eyes Wild Girl's look of affection startled me and yet at the same time stirred up a flicker of reassurance. The butterflies fluttered my belly. A pleasant weakness overtook me, even though I experienced a strength I had never felt before. Wild Girl rolled onto her back and exposed her furry white underbelly while her back legs spread like a turkey waiting to be stuffed. I quickly looked away. Sensing my embarrassment, she sprang to her feet. We both turned away, me to find my tiger bed and her trotting away to tend to her business of monitoring her territory.

Mom had placed my bed in the patch of sunshine by the long window and I curled up in it. Exhaustion overtook me. Resting my chin on my paws I mused as I gazed out at the green landscape.

Only an hour ago I had been convinced Mom was done with me. No one could have made me differently. How could I have been so certain the trip to the vet was my last ride? And what about my certainty that Petunia's outcry had been one of disgust and that I was just Mom's disposable clown? I now realized all my distress was rooted in a strong case of self-pity. The only one who had sold me short was me.

No longer high on the peanut butter paste that Mom had been feeding me for pain, my head was clear. I concentrated on the view from the long window. The seed for my pathetic viewpoint of myself had been planted years ago when I first arrived at Mom's grooming shop -- when people started calling me a rescue -- a wounded soul.

I had bought the story like a tasty treat. I'd gone along. Playing the helpless card was an excusable way to avoid facing the risks waiting for me if I ventured out to find my family and Petunia. I may have made bad choices in the past, but now I could see with new eyes. Could it be that I am worthwhile and loveable? Call me a throwaway, a rescue, whatever you want, but I will not answer to those names anymore.

My only hope is that Mom would understand when I leave on my hunt for Petunia. I wished I could make Mom understand I cannot abandon my quest. I love Petunia. I should have gone back for her.

I owe amends to Mom too. I shuddered as I remembered sinking my teeth into her hand. I should never have bitten her. And yet Mom had not even mentioned it. I think she understood how upset I was but that's no excuse. And somehow, I think she will also understand that I have to do this. I hope so. I wish I could promise her I will return home afterward. But what I was about to do was dangerous. I may not be able to keep that promise.

With my new outlook on life, I was also ready for the laughing blackbirds, but they were nowhere in sight. I growled. Before I begin my hunt for Petunia, I might just hang around long enough to set those birds straight. I will begin my new lease on life with a new attitude and a clean slate. That's all I can do.

CHAPTER TWENTY-EIGHT

The sun's warmth lured me from my musings. On the river road below, I caught sight of those damned blackbirds. They had not gone far. They circled the carcass of a baby squirrel who had lost its race across the asphalt while bigger turkey vultures feasted on the little creature's remains. The gluttonous black birds upset that they must wait their turn, crouched in a line on a tree limb above the accident scene like marathon runners waiting for the shot from a starter's gun.

From inside I couldn't hear the birds' rakish caws or the demonic buzzing of the flies swarming the accident scene. At last, the turkey vultures ate their fill, and one by one took their perch in the nearby trees. When only one of the big birds remained and sensing their turn was near the black bird's cacophony increased. Even I could hear them. Dropping from the tree, they landed and circled the tiny carcass ready to rush in and take the carnivore's place.

It was then I caught a movement. In the thick bushes on the roadside, the baby squirrel's distraught mother fretted. Her mouth quivered as did her upright tail. I could only imagine the heartache she felt. She refused to abandon her kit. Taking advantage of the small gap during the shift change between the raptors and the ravens, she skittered across the road to rescue her fallen kit.

With sudden alarm, the blackbirds rose. Never the sort to confront live prey, they swooped and pecked at the mother only to drive her away while she frantically jerked and pulled her lifeless charge safely into the shrubbery.

Mom crossed my mind and a wrenching pain shot through my insides. I hoped she would not have to go through the same as the mama squirrel if something happened to me on my quest. I shrugged the thought. There was no other way. I had to go.

When all is said and done, when I die, however, I die, I will leave knowing I did the right thing or at least died trying. I turned from the window. I didn't know how many lives I had left but I wasn't going on to the next one without cleaning up the messes I had made in this one. Good intentions. That's what matters in life.

Rested, I rose from my tiger bed ready to take advantage of my new freedom and attitude. My Harley mouse lay in my path. Like an ice hockey left winger, I batted it down the hall and into Mom's office. I jumped onto her lap as she clacked away on her laptop.

Leaning back in her chair Mom snugged me against her chest while she kissed me on the top of my head. "Aren't you the frisky one?"

I smelled the scabbed-over wound on her hand where I had bitten her. Letting out an apologetic chirp I squirmed out of her clutches and hopped on the desk and gave her my best expectant stare.

"Do you want to put your harness on and go for a walk?" Of course, I did. Not the harness part, but I had to tolerate it to go outside.

I followed her into the mud room. She snatched my harness and lead from where they hung next to her jacket. Kneeling, she pulled it over my head and snugged it around my torso. Slipping into her jacket she flung open the door and we headed down to the lower patio.

The fresh pine air and sunshine stirred my senses, and I began my usual investigation of my surroundings padding along the pavers that led around the back to the pond. Wild Girl's mark was everywhere but I saw no sign of her.

I paused at the waterfall. The rivulets trickled over the rocks and splashed into the pond. Like a melody, gentle patter chanted a prayer which made me think about another nap. I led Mom past the waterfall and up some roughhewn wooden steps which I had never ventured before. The path curved around and behind a curtain of draping grape vines. I dared to peek around the wall of big leaves.

Unseen from below an alcove opened up. Filtered sunshine created shadows across its earthen floor. I ventured inside and Mom followed. The rich black earth was cool to my paws as they crunched upon the fallen leaves underfoot. This was my kind of place. A hushing breeze whispered a plea for quiet contemplation. Little stars of light pranced across the cushiony dirt floor like playful kittens inviting me to sit for a while.

Through a gap in the grapevine curtain, our bedroom window peered up at us. And when I raised my gaze over our house rooftop, a world of green landscape opened up. I could see forever.

As was her habit, Wild Girl appeared from nowhere. She moseyed up to me, butted her head against my cheek, and sat down beside me. I was surprised when Mom didn't shoot her away. Together we all studied the sparkles of sunshine dancing around us.

CHAPTER TWENTY-NINE

The cat gods had thoughtfully endowed the feline species with an unending ability for patience and meditation which the human God had overlooked bestowing on his species. Thus, Mom grew restless with my drawn-out introspections over a blade of grass. Did she think the world might pass her by if she lingered too long? After a few moments, she interrupted my pensive investigation of the shadowy alcove and its intriguing energy by tugging on my leash. "Let's head inside," she said. "I'm not getting anything done while you contemplate the meaning of life."

I sighed reluctantly and succumbed to her schedule. I couldn't complain. She had tolerated mine over the years. She made living life at the end of a leash tolerable and dignified. I will forever be grateful for that. As she led me from the alcove I looked back over my shoulder. Watching me leave Wild Girl remained where she sat and waved goodbye with a swish of her tail.

Back inside the mud room, Mom unhooked my leash just when a commotion on our private road distracted her. B=Red flashing brake lights from an SUV towing a trailer lit up our driveway. "Someone must be lost," Mom said as she slung my leash on its hook, pushed open the screen door, and stepped outside to investigate.

She was halfway down the drive when it dawned on me that the latch on the door had not clicked shut. There it was. My chance to begin my quest. That familiar sliver of sunlight signaled the door was ajar. So soon? I only hesitated a minute.

Once you know exactly what you want, make the decision, and go after it. With love and passion, you will find your path will reveal itself and there will be nothing that can stop you. Dad's idiom, one of many which always seemed to pop into my head at the right moment spurred me on. I knew what I wanted and what I needed to do. My heart raced. It was now or never.

I squeezed through the opening, my paws barely touching the steps as I flew down them. As I landed on the second to last stair my injured shoulder gave way. I tumbled onto the walkway and rolled off the pavers and into the dirt.

I shot a glance down the drive. Had Mom seen me fall? Nope. She was already occupied with a woman who was exiting her vehicle.

Squeals of delight and laughter echoed down the drive as Mom recognized her friend and they hugged. "Carol! I didn't know you were coming! You should have called."

I scrambled to my feet and tested my bum leg. I was good to go. I dashed into the shrubbery alongside the driveway and hid.

The thick-waisted woman stood beside her R.V. beaming with pride as Mom admired it. "It's called a Casita," her friend explained.

My ears pricked alert at the familiar voice.

Mom stretched up on her toes and peeked in the RV's small window. "Oh Carol, it's so cute. And so small. But just right for you and Scarlett Petunia.

Scarlett Petunia?

"Would you like to see inside?" Carol didn't wait for an answer. Keys in hand, she pulled out a step, unlocked the door, and swung it open. The little trailer swayed as the two friends disappeared inside.

Mom's and her friend's tittering and laughter floated outside through the Casita's open door. "It's warm in here. Let me squeeze by. I'll just crank open the window." Carol said. More gaiety danced out the open door followed by the muffled shuffling of feet as the little house rocked and rolled.

A breeze caught the stale air from the camper's interior and carried it across the drive to where I hid. Raising my nose, I caught ahold of a scent. I sniffed the air again. My breath quickened. The scent was *her scent*. My heartbeat took up a forgotten rhythm and my tummy butterflies danced with delight. I choked back a cry of recognition. Carol's Scarlett Petunia was *my Petunia*! She was here!

I wanted to dash across the driveway. But I held back. As I fought the urge my heart screamed, *why hesitate*? Like a swarm of flies, fear and doubts buzzed in my head.

Had Petunia lived so long as a foolish dream inside my head that I couldn't tell reality from fantasy? Until now that was all Petunia was to me -- a fantasy. But it *was* Petunia. She was not a ghost. She was flesh and blood. I shivered.

But was I ready? Her real live presence meant not only the chance to renew our love for one another but also it meant facing my failures to protect her and take care of her that I thought I had buried.

She was so close. Yet still, I remained rooted, unable to move. What was wrong with me now? Was this another one of my bouts of confusion? I growled. No. Not now!

CHAPTER THIRTY

Mom's and Carol's muffled spurts of giggles drifted across the driveway in waves. Curiosity urged me closer. I sprinted from my hiding place, across the driveway to the Casita, and hid behind a tire.

Carol made smoochy noises. "Petunia took to our new life on wheels like she's been a gypsy all her life." I imagined her kissing her Scarlett Petunia, *my Petunia*, on her dark beauty smudge. A pang of jealousy shot through me.

"Didn't you sweetheart?" More mushy sounds. "You're Mama's baby."

Mom probably grinned politely at her friend. She was not the mooshy-mooshy type like Carol. The hell with my doubts. I burst from my hiding place and hopped onto the Casita's step. Scratching at the screen door I let out a loud meow.

Mom's voice smiled. Who's knocking? Is that you, Sportster?" A ruckus followed as the little house rocked and rolled. The girl's giggles and laughter flew outside when they pushed the screen door open. More hilarity. Their bodies tangled up as they scrambled aside when I hopped inside.

"Sportster!" Mom's voice was scolding but she was still laughing. "What are you doing out here?"

I sprang up and into the tiny house on wheels. Before I could even catch my breath, Petunia had squeezed through the women's tangled feet and found her way to me.

Oblivious to the women's merriment, Petunia and I stood face to face at a loss as to what to do next.

Go to her! Go to her! Tell her you love her. Tell her she's the one!

The blackbirds appeared out of nowhere hawking their doubts and discontent. But this time the electric energy pulsing between Petunia and me overruled. Their heckling faded to only that of a bothersome ghost of gnats on a windy day.

I stepped up to Petunia and pressed my cheek against hers. She closed her eyes.

A swooning roar erupted from Mom and Carol. "Ooooh! Look at the love bugs!" Carol clapped her hands and giggled Mom fell back against the sofa.

Oblivious to the flurry of delight from the women, Petunia rolled onto her back.

Another "Ah! So cute!" from the giddy chorus line.

I crouched beside Petunia, nibbling her ears and her neck. My pulse throbbed faster and faster until a stomach cramp brought everything to a halt when I sniffed at an area of exposed skin. Rough to my touch, an ugly scar. Like a red flag, it reminded me of the gaping wound so long ago that I had so tenderly licked and nursed after the rottweiler's attack. Mixed emotions swept over me making me lightheaded. I pulled away but my mind had already raced back to the scene.

A violent trembling shook through me, not from lust, but like it had after the Rottweiler's vicious attack on Petunia. My mind thrust me back into the memory, pushing and dragging Petunia's nearly lifeless body until I reached the safety of our den.

I was so young, so full of love, and crazy with worry for her. I didn't know what to do. I knew her wounds were life-threatening. A paralyzing panic grabbed ahold of me. And then?

It was so long ago I had forgotten. Dad's steady voice talked me through my terror. It was as if he were beside me, but I can't recall ever actually seeing him. But he was there. As if I were there, I could hear his voice. *"You know what to do, Son. It's going to be okay."*

I remember I didn't believe him. How could he know anything? He had left me and my family to our own devices and look how that had turned out. I had argued, "Petunia's going to die. I didn't protect her. It's my fault. ". But even though he wasn't physically there, he had read my thoughts. *"You know what to do, son. Trust your instincts."*

I had wanted to cry and run away. My heart pounded as it was doing now as I stood before Petunia. Back then I had been unable to ignore the strong faith Dad had in me. He made me believe everything was going to be okay. His voice, like a blanket, wrapped me in newfound peace and confidence. I knew I had to at least try. And I did. I found the courage and stuck it out. I didn't give up.

❀ ❀ ❀ ❀ ❀ ❀

And here she is alive and healthy standing before me. All these years, believing she was dead. Believing I was at fault. Such a heavy burden for a young cat to carry. But now I know. She had not died. Maybe I even saved her life.

I came back. Petunia's tail swished seductively back and forth waiting for me to come back from my trip to the past. She rolled onto her stomach and stared at me. Flashing me a long slow blink she came up to me and caressed her cheek against mine. My legs felt like noodles.

I inched alongside Petunia. We doled out playful bites to each other as we rolled and tumbled on the floor. Carol poked Mom with her elbow. "This is embarrassing. Shall we give them privacy?"

Mom smiled down at us. "Do you think they knew each other from another life? Or maybe it's love at first sight. Do cats fall in love at first sight?"

Carol shook her head. "I don't know, but whatever it is, they are, as we say in LA., definitely an item."

Mom grinned at her friend. "How about we go into town and have a late lunch, give them some alone time? When we get back you can rest up or take a nap while I finish up a few things in my office. I'll bet you're probably tired from the long drive. And then tonight, we'll have dinner around the firepit. How does that sound?"

Hanging her coffee mug on a hook and wiping her hands on a dishtowel, Carol gathered up her purse. "Lunch and a nap sound great. And then tomorrow I'll be ready for the five-star tour of the town."

Mom's little car crunched over the gravel as she backed out of the driveway. The women's muffled conversation faded as the little car picked its way down to the river road and sped toward town.

Petunia and I were alone.

CHAPTER THIRTY-ONE

A couch under the window encompassed the width of the trailer affording a full view of the driveway. Over the back of the sofa, Petunia's mom had draped a blanket over the back probably to protect it from the cat hair. When the women closed the door behind them, Petunia took her perch on the back of the sofa and watched her mom leave.

I shrugged off the aching reminder that we were both old cats and followed after her. Careful not to embarrass myself and fall, I leaped. My joints cried out. I faltered only a bit from dizziness which I blamed on Petunia's closeness.

As I sat down beside her, she purred loudly and rubbed her nose against mine. Her actions reassured me she had never doubted my feelings for her. And yet I felt compelled to ask anyway. While we both gazed out the window, I braved the question that had haunted me for years. "Did you think I had abandoned you?" Petunia leaned into me, purring even louder, and placed her paw on mine. Relieved, I confessed. "I wanted to find you, too."

So, Carol found Petunia near death's door and rescued her. My heart welled up, knowing that neither of us had planned to separate. It had been divine intervention that had intruded on our hopes and dreams.

All these years I couldn't bear the thought that she might think I had abandoned her. So, I imagined her dead, or at least hating me. "Pretty much the same thing happened to me. So, I understand," I returned Petunia's affections licking her all over with a desperate eagerness.

We dozed in the quiet of our surroundings until a Blue Jay's punctuated statements about his latest commentary on life woke me. I checked on Petunia. She continued to sleep, exhausted from her travels. Outside, a deer and her fawn with their stilted gait tiptoed down to the river.

I climbed down from the couch and investigated the accommodations. I found Petunia's litter box, did my business, and then checked out her food bowl. Only a few kibbles remained, but I wasn't hungry. I didn't think I would ever have to eat again because a feeling of peace, like the quiet after a snowfall, enveloped me. I needed nothing. My life was complete.

A crisp fall breeze floated through the RV's screen door, so I returned to Petunia where the sun penetrated the window and warmed us. Outside, golden leaves sprinkled on the ground.

I exhaled a big sigh and rested my chin on my paws. This was how I wanted to live out my life, sharing my time with someone I love, and I know loves me. My heart swelled at the thought. Life's circumstances may have stolen our youth and a chance for a family, but I couldn't help wondering what it would have been like if things had been different.

Movement along the driveway drew my attention. Wild Girl was returning from her trip to the river, her footfall, a bit heavier, was more of a waddle. She spotted me watching from the Casita's window and paused. For a moment I wanted to go out and tell her of my good fortune in finding Petunia. I loved how Wild Girl always liked being with me. But just then a sleek black cat which looked like he had just come from Cinderella's ball with his white mustache and paws appeared from the thick brush and joined her. A new wild cat in the territory? Or did he live in one of the neighboring homes? The two acknowledged one another with a couple of casual sniffs and a twitch of their tails. They became engrossed with grooming each other.

Like a bright lightbulb flashing on, the scene suddenly blindsided me. Their simplistic admiration of each other, their ease and comfort with one another triggered an understanding that I didn't know I was seeking. I hissed as a stab of jealousy startled me. Her waddle. Their familiarity. Their 'knowing' of each other. It all made sense. She was in a family way. Wild Girl had someone in her life.

Feeling a chill, I sat up stiffly and wrapped my tail tight around my front paws. Of course, she did. A melancholy hung in the silence. I tried to breathe in the lush beauty of the landscape and smell the salty air creeping up the river from the ocean to alleviate the feeling of loss. This is the way of life. When I exhaled a rush of acceptance crashed over me like a wave over a rock. A keen razor of remorse sliced through me releasing a cry of regret.

Mom had made her feelings clear long ago when I was too young to understand. "The world does not need more kittens. And certainly not with a wild cat." I disagreed. But my opinion didn't matter. Mom had "fixed" that argument. Even though I was innocent I knew after the trip to the People's Humane Army, there would be no family for me. I was only six months old.

The air seeping up the river carried the lyrics of a sad song I had heard long ago, "This nearly was mine." I couldn't give Wild Girl a family.

My best memories are of the times with my siblings. Playing and cheering each other. Embracing the thrills as we tested our freedom and ventured past the limits of our den. Those were the days.

Family love has been sorely discounted these days. Sure, we may have had our spats, but we taught each other boundaries. We learned that our behavior affected others. We learned that if one of us were in a tight spot, or danger and too far from the den, we had his back. You stand by family -- you puff up, arch your back, and help them find their way home. I sighed. I will never have a family.

The melancholy song of the river reached a crescendo. From the time Wild Girl and I met I had avoided her desires, scoffing them off because Mom would never approve of my relationship with a wild cat, kittens, or no kittens. I kept my condition secret from Wild Girl, but I think she guessed.

So, if it couldn't be me to give her a family, I was glad the new Tuxedo Tom in town could. Wild Girl would be a good mother. I glanced back at Petunia where she lay sleeping. There would be no babies with Petunia and me, either.

CHAPTER THIRTY-TWO

The afternoon passed quickly. Before I knew it Mom's little car entered the drive and crunched across the gravel into the carport. Petunia came alert and her eyes popped wide open. When she recognized her mom and mine slamming car doors and rustling paper bags, she gave a quick shake to sluff off her deep sleep and bounded off the couch and to the door.

Mom and Carol flung open the door and hefting shopping bags they squeezed into the little trailer. My Mom's eyes followed Petunia as she rubbed against Carol's ankles chirping and purring loudly. While Petunia wove figure eights around and between Carol's feet, my mom glanced at Petunia with an adoring smile she only used on me. And then, she voiced aloud what my startled heart was thinking. "What's this? She's ignoring Sportster. Is the affair over before it started?"

Carol laughed but I didn't find Mom's statement amusing. I let out a deep heartfelt meow. When no one even paused from pulling their trinkets from their shopping bags I shrank away and pretended to gaze out the window.

Petunia hopped onto the counter, plopped beside her mom, and became engrossed with the paper sack her mom had brought home for her pleasure.

Frustrated by Petunia's dismissal I meowed again and jumped down from the sofa. This time Mom caught my eye. "Oooh baby! I'm so sorry. Is she snubbing you?" She scooped me up and proceeded to smother me with kisses. I hated her gushing over me, especially in front of other people. She treated me like a helpless kitten. I squirmed to get down.

" It's okay little buddy. You're still the best. I love you so much!" Planting one last kiss on my nose she released me, and I sprang down. Turning my back on everyone, I stood at the door. This time I howled, demanding to go home.

"Okay! Okay! We're going." After giving Carol a big hug, Mom slipped her shopping bag on her arm and picked me up. "You have a nice nap. Rest up. We'll do burgers at the barbeque for dinner and sit around the firepit afterward and have hot cocoa. What do you think? About six?"

Carol nodded as she spooned Fancy Feast into Petunia's bowl. "That sounds wonderful."

Engrossed with doting on her mom Petunia didn't notice Mom and me heading out the door. I refused to look back as we left.

❀ ❀ ❀ ❀ ❀ ❀

Back in the house, after Mom had settled into her recliner and put her feet up, I curled up on her lap. "What a busy day." Smiling down at me as she ran her hand over my back and scratched my chin. "I have to admit I was a little jealous when you were making google eyes at Scarlett."

I jerked my head around and gazed up at her with big eyes. *Yeah? Really?*

She giggled. "Did you understand what I just said?"

Scoffing off her question I turned away. We cats may not be capable of talking but that doesn't mean we don't understand. People think they understand cats, but they only see us from their lofty human perspective. I hate to say it, but their viewpoint is quite shallow. We're always being misunderstood.

Brows raised Mom gave me an indignant look. "Yes! I'm not afraid to admit it. I was jealous!" Her mouth turned pouty. "It was like you didn't care about me anymore."

I made the mistake of glancing back at her. Now her face wore a frown like it does when I get overly excited and bite too hard.

"But it's okay. Scarlett's a pretty kitty." She raised her brows again and gave me a tilted smile. "You have good taste."

Mom's silly attitude rubbed me the wrong way. Was she making fun of me? Sure, I know it looked like Petunia had shoved me to the curb just to get to Carol but she was just hungry. And I know I'm always hungrier when I can see the shiny bottom of the dish. And anyway, I'm the one who licked her dish clean.

"I'm glad it's Scarlett you like. And I'm relieved you've given up the idea of running off with Wild Girl."

What? No! It wasn't like that at all!

"I don't know what I would have done if you had run away. I would have worried every minute knowing you were living in the wild."

My heart ached. I wanted to tell her that I never intended on leaving her and that I was always going to come back Her expression darkened. Tears welled in her eyes threatening to flow. I reached up and gave her a reassuring head butt.

How could I make her understand? Wild Girl's just a friend.

On the patio below Carol tended the firepit while in the kitchen Mom removed the hamburger patties from the grill and in the kitchen dished the salad into bowls. Sliding the burgers onto their buns, she scanned the array of napkins, utensils, and paper plates filling the two trays, and wiped her hands on a dishtowel. She glanced down at me and said, "Okay, everything's ready." She balanced a platter on each arm, and I followed her down the stairs to the patio.

Seeing Mom with her arms full Carol sprang from her camp chair and grabbed a platter. "Boy! I could smell those burgers from down here! I'm so hungry." Flames stretched out of the firepit crackling as they sparked in the dimming light of evening. Carol gazed at the landscape reaching past the road below and stopped at the river's shore.

On the opposite bank, a solid wall of trees climbed straight up and touched the gray evening sky. Cottony puffs hung in the once baby blue sky which was now being painted pink and gray by the setting sun. "This is so rustic. It's like we're camping. Look at the clouds creeping up the river."

Mom smiled at Carol. "That's fog moving upriver from the harbor. The first evening I spent here I thought it was it was a forest fire." She handed Carol her plate. "But then it dawned on me, it wasn't smoke, but the fog."

I skimmed over the patio area looking for Petunia. She must have stayed in the trailer. When Petunia and I visited that afternoon, she made it clear she had no desire to go outside. "It's not that I'm scared, it's just that I have everything I need." But I think she was scared. I think that Rottweiler attack affected her more than she wanted to admit.

I hopped up onto the lounge chair so the heat of the fire could warm my bones. My eyelids began to droop. As I drifted off, I wished Petunia would have joined us. But I'll convince her I can take care of her now. I'm not a kitten anymore.

I caught my breath and my eyes popped open. Like a bandit

coming to steal my confidence self-doubt raised its head. *YOU'RE going to protect her? Who saved you from the eagle attack? And the angry raccoon? When was the last time you had to hunt? Or sleep out in the rain?*

I scratched my ear and dismissed the demeaning accusations. Funny but they seemed so silly now. Everything WAS going to be okay. My new attitude startled me. Everything had changed since what I thought was my 'last trip" to the veterinarian.

I stood up on the chaise lounge, stretched, and gathered my thoughts. After circling to get more comfortable I plopped back down and stared into the fire. The heat soothed my aged body like a bomb. Carol and Mom's usual, incessant chatter slowed as they ate their burgers. All was good. The flickering flames danced as they sprinkled stardust into the velvety darkness.

CHAPTER THIRTY-THREE

"I've got hot water for tea if you like. Or there's coffee," Mom said as she collected Carol's paper plate and tossed it and hers into the fire and then gathered up the trays.

"I'll take tea. It's a little late for coffee. It'll keep me awake." Carol stood, taking one of the trays from Mom. "Here, I'll give you a hand."

The darkness had laid a blanket of silence over the area by the time the girlfriends returned. They huddled into their camping chairs, cupped their mugs, and stared into the hypnotizing firelight.

After a long pause, Mom broke the serene spell. "Tomorrow we'll go to the harbor and take a walk on the beach. And afterward, if you want, we can take a drive through the Redwoods. It's such a magical experience."

"That sounds great." Carol gave a sideways nod toward me curled up on the lounge chair. "If you want you can leave Sportster with Scarlett tomorrow. They can keep each other company while we're gone."

Mom glanced at me too. "That'll be nice. I worry about him these days. He's getting so feeble."

"I know. My Petunia is too. When she tries to jump up on the counter she sometimes misses and falls." Carol's face slackened into a frown. "It's so sad to watch. Probably humiliating, too. Cats are so proud, you know? Every time it happens it reminds me; I will not have her forever."

Mom leaned into the fire, her elbows leaning on her knees and her hands clasping her mug. After a long pause, she spoke in a low tone almost a whisper. The forbidden words that I had only heard others say about their pets now escaped my mom's lips. "It's going to be so hard when he's gone."

Gone? My ears perked. *No!* If she's talking about me leaving to search for Petunia surely, she knows I don't have to do that now. I'm not going anywhere. Petunia is going to stay and live with us.

"When I think of all the places we've been together. All the times he's comforted me." Mom wrung her hands. "I know he's only a cat, but when a cat is all you have…" Her voice drifted off.

I swallowed hard. The realization hit me. A painful lump in my throat landed like a rock in my gut. She wasn't talking about me *leaving*-leaving. She was talking about leaving *for good*! The silence turned heavy as we all became lost in our thoughts.

I sprang from the chaise lounge and landed with a clumsy thud on the ground. Shaking off my embarrassment I leaped into Mom's lap. I pressed up against her and wished desperately she could understand. *Hey, I'm not going anywhere.*

Mom's watery eyes moved over me. Giving me a hard hug, she took my paw. "You always know when I'm sad."

Carol sipped her tea as she looked on. "Ah, what a brave little guy." She leaned back in her chair. "He's brave because you're brave. He's adventurous because you're an adventurer." Then she added. "Petunia's a stay-at-home cat 'cause her mom is." Then Carol patted her stomach. "She's even got a few extra pounds like her mom." They giggled and Carol went on. "I think because they're rescues, they're overly grateful to us."

Giving me a tired smile, Mom's shoulders sagged. Her voice seemed to cry as she spoke. "The vet said his incontinence is common for a cat his age.' She slumped like a soggy rag, her voice so low I wondered if Carol heard. "It's a sign his kidneys are beginning to fail."

A teardrop landed on my paw. I ignored another painful lump forming in my throat and gave Mom's hand a hard nudge.

"How am I going to handle it?" She gulped. "When he's gone?" The deep ache in Mom's voice raked threw me like claws on a screen door. I had to find a way to assure her, tell her that no matter what, I would always be with her.

Carol curled her fingers around Mom's hand which held my paw and she squeezed. "You'll deal with it, girlfriend. Just like all the other struggles you've faced."

Mom's hooded eyes met her friend's as her face contorted with emotion. She forced a smile. "Except for the four months he was lost in the Olympic Forest he's been everywhere with me." Then she swatted at her tears leaking freely down her cheeks.

I tried to push away the pangs of guilt as I remembered those four months. Plagued in fear and loneliness I had cursed her for abandoning me.

Mom's face warped and her voice turned flat. "Everyone thought he was dead."

Carol scooted her chair closer, draped an arm over Mom's fallen shoulders, and resumed patting her hand. "But he wasn't." Then Carol showered me with a caring smile. "Look at him," she said. "He's not dead now." Her voice cheered. "And he's met Scarlett, so I don't think he's going to give up anytime soon. "

Mom wiped her chin with a Kleenex Carol pulled magically from her pocket. Forcing a tired smile, she leaned against her friend. And then she cupped my face in her hands, and kissed me all over, my nose, my mouth, my eyes, and each cheek. "I'll always be there for you, my little buddy." She sat up stiffly and drew in a deep cleansing breath. Blinking she put me down and stretched rose to her feet. "I don't know what's wrong with me."

She swatted at her wet cheeks one last time and nodded toward the fog on the river. "The reality is creeping up on me like that fog." Bolstering herself she crossed her arms. Letting loose a shiver she rubbed her forearms briskly. "As you said, I'll get through it." She shook her head and thought, but afterward?

Carol stood beside Mom patting her back. They both stared into the fire as if it held the answers. After several moments Carol broke the trance and gave Mom a questioning look. "Do you plan on getting another cat? A kitten would fill the big hole Sportster's going to leave in your heart?"

Lost in unwanted thoughts, Mom didn't look up.

"Did I ever tell you about my friend Melody? Her property butted up against Dad's. Melody and her husband had horses, so they kept feral cats in their hay barn. One day one of the wild cats ventured up toward their house. Usually, they didn't come that close. This was a mama cat and her teats almost dragged the ground. Melody said she had a litter somewhere. Anyway, when the mama cat got close enough Melody saw she had a kitten in her mouth. Then she just dropped it on the doormat at the kitchen door and ran back towards the barn."

Mom looked up her brow furrowed. "The mama cat gave your friend one of her kittens?"

Carol grinned. "Yes! Have you ever heard of anything like that? "

Mom stared back into the fire. "Maybe the kitten was sick."

Carol shook her head. "Nope. It was a healthy kitten. She still has it." Carol looked around the area. "Didn't you say there is a feral cat that hangs around? " Mom raised her brow and sighed. "I know what you're suggesting but I don't think so."

What? I could not believe it. I'm not even gone yet?! And the woman was suggesting Mom replace me like a ratty toy?

But the question was out there.

CHAPTER THIRTY-FOUR

As fast as my indignation flared, it faded just as quickly. Like a reading light, the moon shined down on the scene washing me with a faith that no one could challenge. I didn't know what to do for Mom, but I knew everything was going to be okay.

I no longer had to live my life with my chest puffed out, my back arched, and a switching tail to prove I was somebody. I no longer had to spend my energy covering up who I thought I was—a throwaway cat.

I was no longer worried this might be the day I lost my grip on my bravado, or if it was the day that someone might see past my disguise. The gloom and doom of someday facing the cages of the People's Humane Army had haunted me for so long. The possibility was always waiting around the next corner. It was never a matter of *if I would* fall, but when.

And now? It turns out the trip to the vet *was* a *no-return trip*, but only for my pompous ego. In its place, I was now enjoying tremendous peace and serenity. I will look for my pompous ego lying in the ditch somewhere along the river road the next time we go into town.

Were the cat gods responsible for my new faith? I will never really know for sure. All I know is without my ego, a new world has opened up. I suddenly had everything I needed.

Petunia had come to *me*. I no longer faced the treacherous journey I had secretly dreaded. One which certainly would have been the end of me. *That* would have been my last trip. And most important, I no longer have to leave Mom alone.

My new understanding and humility filled me with a fuzzy feeling inside like wearing a warm coat. And the crows who haunted me and pointed out my unworthiness? They must have gone south. Without their cackling lyrics harping in my ears, I no longer doubt who I am.

I know the real end is coming. But I also know Mom will be okay. And I will be too.

Even if Mom gets a new kitten.

Mom rustled me from my reverie and gathered me in her arms. Standing she addressed Carol. "I had fun today." Giving Carol a one-armed hug she added, "Sleep tight in that cozy little home of yours. And let me know when you're ready in the morning. We can go out for breakfast and then I'll show you around."

"That will be great." Carol beamed down at me and scratched me behind the ears. "Sportster! I'm so glad you got to meet my Petunia. You two will have a lovely day tomorrow while your mom and I go exploring." She wrapped Mom and me in a group hug, said good night, and headed out to her little home on wheels.

As Mom carried me into the house, Scarlett sat as a silhouette in the Casita's window. Was she waiting for me… or Carol?

❁ ❁ ❁ ❁ ❁ ❁

After mindlessly puttering in the kitchen, with a heavy footfall Mom headed for her recliner and sank into it. With a ragged sigh, she pressed her palms to her face. Her muffled breaths gushed out in ragged puffs.

Alarmed, I lumbered over to her and hopped into her lap. Even though my body nagged at me with an exhausted fiery ache, I ignored it. With a comforting mew, I nudged her elbow.

Dropping her hands, she swiped them on her jeans and gathered me up. The corners of her watery eyes creased from her tender smile. Her eyes trailed over me in a way that melted me. A fragile silence hung between us. A minute dragged by like a lifetime. And then, her eyes clouded with aching desperation, and she told me what she had told me so many, many times before, "I love you too, my little buddy." But this time she said it like it might be the last.

Her words unarmed me, unwinding something inside. The TV flickered and I swallowed hard. Again, I mewed in a small voice.

She sagged like a wet rag, and tears flooded her cheeks. She hugged me tight, but not too tight, as if she knew how much I hurt. Tears dampened a few fly-aways of her hair that were stuck to her cheeks. They soaked my fur too, but I didn't pull away.

CHAPTER THIRTY-FIVE

As the TV droned on, I curled up in Mom's lap and I sank into a deep sleep.

I was a young and healthy cat again. Petunia sprang from behind a tree taking me by surprise. Playing the part of the big tough Tom, hair on end, I leaped high into the air over a field of clover. Chirping with glee I made a solid landing in front of her.

Laughing, she scampered across the fragrant, thick-carpeted field of flowers. Lightheaded and carefree, I high-tailed after her, my heart swelling with the promise of a love-filled future.

In the middle of the field, she came to an abrupt halt and spun around. Braking, I slid on my haunches, but couldn't stop. To avoid slamming into her I squeezed my eyes shut and again I leaped high. Water droplets tickled my nose and ears. Opening my eyes, I found myself on a cushiony cloud. I could see forever.

Petunia's laughter echoed from below. I peered down to see her glancing this way and that as she wondered where I had gone. I laughed so loud she looked up. Seeing me, her face lit up with wonderment. But something caught her attention and her focus shifted past me.

Spooked I attempted to spin around, but instead, I floated lazily around like a rogue balloon. I tried to bolt but that was not effective either. On a cloud, there is no traction.

I recognized the husky purr before I saw his loose smile coming through the mist. It was Dad! He floated toward me. He was younger than I remembered. A charged energy sparked around us like lightning break dancing in the clouds, yet I was unafraid. I bounded toward him. As I sprinted up to him, he gave me a brusque head bump and looked me over like he used to do when I was a kitten, as if I were a precious gem to him. I stretched my chin up sitting even taller, pride bursting in my chest. I had forgotten how good he made me feel.

He heard my unspoken questions as I hammered him for answers.

"I've always been with you, son." His eyes softened with understanding. "I know you're worried about your mom. But there is no need. You will find a way to help her make it through your transition. Me and the boys have seen to the details." His voice had a lazy morning calmness that erased my concerns. My heart hiccuped at his mention of 'his boys.'

Grandpa, Uncle Tommy, and several of his rough and ragged, unkempt friends were his boys. They spent their lives prowling the streets and countryside, bringing cats and kittens who have lost their way home to their families. His boys called their themselves 'Crook's Cats–Fighting for Freedom.'

He hitched a thumb in Petunia's direction on the ground below. "Someone is waiting for you."

But when I looked down Petunia was gone. Wild Girl sat in her place placidly grooming one paw then another, pausing now and then to sniff a blossom. I shot Dad a questioning look.

He waggled an eyebrow and a laugh started deep in his throat and then burst forth as if he let loose of its reins. "Sometimes the answers to your problems are right under your nose."

I looked down again at Wild Girl and grunted. What could she do to help Mom? Mom doesn't like wild cats. You already know that. And Wild Girl would never want to live with... Anyway, she's pregnant. No one wants a cat AND kittens." My mind swirled as if too were vanishing into the clouds. What are you suggesting? My words diffused like smoke in the surrounding mist. I swung back to face Dad. His image, like my arguments, had faded into thin air.

"Wait! Don't go!"

Only cloud shadows remained. But his voice cut through the haze like an order. "You have things to wrap up down there. Then you can move on to your new life adventure. But don't worry I'll be around when you're ready."

I jerked awake.

CHAPTER THIRTY-SIX

A quick survey found me not in the clouds but still on Mom's lap. She lay her chin on her chest, asleep in her chair. Her hand still rested on my back. I panicked. I needed to use my litter box and *did not* want to lose control before I reached it. I tried to slip out from under her warm hand, but it was heavy, and I did not want to wake her. I'd slept too long, and every joint protested.

A soft curl of a smile moved across Mom's face as she stirred awake. "Want to get up?" Gently she slid her hand under me and lifted me to the floor. I rocked unsteadily, and then fully awake, I flattened my ears remembering my dilemma. With a reassuring grin from Mom and a deep breath, I plodded toward the mud room.

The trip to the litter box relieved my fear of an accident and loosened my joints. Encouraged, I slipped into the kitchen where Mom was making a snack of tortilla chips and guacamole while a cup of tea heated up in the microwave. I angled my gaze in her direction and meowed.

"I know. You want a drink." Bending down she swooped me up, planted a quick kiss on my head, and set me in front of the kitchen faucet. The cool water poured out in a steady stream. As I lapped, I savored the chilling sensation as the liquid slid down my throat and into my tummy. I appreciated the little things these days. When I finished, I watched Mom sprinkle a handful of chips on a platter that held a bowl of guacamole and a teacup.

Her eyes flitted toward me. "You want one?" She held a chip in front of my nose. She knew I liked to lick them. I took a sniff and took a couple of licks. I don't eat chips but liked how their flavor clung to the salt.

"You sure you don't want the chip?" She held it steady.

Maybe. I bit off a piece and tossed it around in my mouth. Nope. I spit it out.

"Well, at least you tried it.' Tossing it in the trash she chuckled. "I don't want it either now that it's all mushy." Lifting the snack plate, she carried it into the living room and set it on the side table. Plopping down into her chair she grabbed the remote and pointed it at the TV. As it flickered to life I sprang onto her lap, climbed across the armrest, and snatched another chip but she pulled the morsel from my mouth.

"Here, I'll hold it for you, so you don't lose it in cushion's crevice."

stepped back onto her lap and proceeded to work on the salty chip until it was soggy. Then clamping down on it I thought I'd taste it again.

Mom yanked it away. "Oh no. You're not going to spit it out on my furniture."

Yeah. I didn't really want it anyway.

❊ ❊ ❊ ❊ ❊ ❊

When I woke again, I caught my breath and I found myself curled up in my tiger bed which Mom had placed on the corner of her bed. I didn't remember how I got there. The morning light lit up the bedroom. I shook my head to clear it, stood, and stretched.

Mom was already puttering around in the bathroom. I guess the whine of the hair dryer woke me. She caught a glimpse of my movement and called out a cheery good morning. "You better get a move on, little buddy. You're going to spend a day with your honey."

I plunked my rear back down on the bed and let out a sigh wondering if I was up to it. I sniffed. Just the lavender aroma of the bedsheets. I gave a silent cheer. I didn't smell like my litter box. I spruced up my fur here and there surprised I wasn't more excited about the visit, but I was still in a funk after listening to Mom's worries last night.

Like I have done for a lifetime I looked on while Mom went on about her morning routine. Her smiling eyes crinkled at the corners when she blew me a kiss as she did now. Dimples creased her cheeks and she grinned. "I love you. Who's the man? You da man."

At first, I just looked on. I didn't like to encourage her. She gets carried away so easily when I do. Except she's going to miss me, you know, when I'm gone. Ignoring my stiffness, I sprang down from the bed and trotted to her. I stretched up, placing my paws on her thigh, and let out a heartfelt chirp. And just as I predicted she pulled me up into her arms and showered me with kisses. Then, setting me down on the floor, she proceeded to shrug into her jeans. "Let's go see Scarlett Petunia."

Why was I dreading the visit? Petunia is all I ever wanted. But deep down I knew how this was going to play out. After yesterday Petunia had made it clear that her devotion to Carol was as strong as mine was to my mom. A hammering round of pain shot through my body at the thought. And I knew the choice I was going to make too. Something twisted at my innards as I came to terms with the reality of our lives. I wobbled with dizziness at the thought of letting go of Petunia.

CHAPTER THIRTY-SEVEN

Mom swung open the Casita's door to find Petunia sitting primly in the doorway. She presented propriety to the world with a big-eyed stare and just the slightest twitch of her tail. Her meow was loud but still dainty enough to send a sweet thrill shooting through me. I squirmed in Mom's arms.

Mom's face softened as she peered down at me. "Okay. Okay." Sitting me down beside her, I sensed no sign of the jealousy she had mentioned yesterday. She watched Petunia rub up against me while I returned her affections with chirps of adoration. She pulled in a deep breath and stepped away from Petunia and me. Smiling at Carol, she leaned in and hugged her friend. "Good morning."

I trailed behind Petunia as she climbed up onto the back of the sofa. We both sniffed in the damp chilly air drifting in through the slightly open window and mixed with the warm, rich coffee aroma and sweet smell of sugar and cinnamon.

Carol nodded toward the kitchen counter "Cinnamon rolls," she said, taking one. "Help yourself. They're still warm."

Mom snatched one up, joined Carol at the dinette, and they began to chatter away over their steamy coffee and savory sweets.

"How did you sleep?" Mom asked as she moaned and inhaled the scent of her pastry.

"Like a baby. It's so quiet here. I didn't even wake up to pee."

Mom laughed easily as she tore off a section of her delicacy. "Now that's a testament." Popping the morsel in her mouth she licked her fingers. "Are you ready for your tour?"

The sun pushed through the fog that hovered over the river. Sunny splotches dotted the ground. Musky steam rose from the leaf-covered soil damp from last night's light shower.

"Yes, ma'am. I can't wait to walk the beach." Carol shoved the leftover sweets into the oven. "There. Out of the paws' reach of our little rascals."

Grabbing her purse and jacket, Carol stepped out of the little trailer. Mom began to follow but hesitated. Turning to me our eyes met. She leaned over the couch and bent down to kiss me. She rubbed her nose against my face and inhaled my scent. Her hugs and kisses lingered longer these days as if she savored every minute we shared. And then she kissed me. "I love you so much." The intensity of her words imprinted onto my soul and would live with me forever in my spirit. After one last peck on the top of my head, heavily she pulled away as if I were a powerful magnet. "Later gator." And she rushed out the door.

When the little car's tires crunched down the driveway and disappeared into the tunnel of trees lining the river road, Petunia turned to me. Purring full blast, she touched her nose to mine and began to groom me. With a steady, strong rhythm her tongue massaged me. I leaned up against her I couldn't get close enough. I rubbed up hard against her, our purrs mingled into a love song,

A Blue Jay fluttered past the window and perched on a nearby tree limb. Although I couldn't translate his chatter, I recognized his greeting. He was the same guy who greeted me on my first day here. He flitted from the limb that he perched on next to the Casita, and still chattering landed on the split rail fence outlining the drive. Hopping and bopping from the fence, he lit on to the ground, back to the fence, and then again to the limb by the Casita's window. He repeated his dance steps until I noticed his display was not just for me but Wild Girl too, who watched nearby.

She sat unmoving with an air of self-assurance. Only her green eyes moved as she followed the Jay's line of flight until he perched on the branch by me. Then, shifting her focus she blinked at me. long and slow. The tip of her tail twitched back and forth in a hypnotic rhythm. I let loose a whisper of a chirp even though I knew she couldn't hear.

Petunia turned to me.

I gave Petunia a nudge of reassurance and then stole another glance out the window, but Wild Girl had gone. The day passed easily. Petunia and I tumbled and pounced as if we were kittens. Wrestling and play-biting, we ate from the same bowl and cat-napped together. By late afternoon we collapsed on the sofa and curled into a combined furball.

And we slept.

CHAPTER THIRTY-EIGHT

I dreamed of soaring with eagles and having no fear. I hovered at the edge of a cloud, breathing in a feast of savory tuna-smelling food. Colorful feathery toys lay before emanating the stimulating scent of catnip stuffed inside each one. Chattering and car doors slamming woke me. Petunia stirred too, as she woke from her curled-up position beside me. Stretching as she stood, she sniffed and nudged me here and there. She licked my face. Then with a shiver, she sat back on her haunches and whispered the slightest mew.

I went to her, sat beside her, and gave her a reassuring nudge. But my gesture went unnoticed because my nose met only air. I almost tripped. I scanned the room. She must have moved. And then I froze.

I saw *myself* still sleeping, curled up among the pillows on the sofa. Petunia's indentation remained on the cushion where she had lain beside me.

Ignoring my clumsiness, Petunia curled up next to my still body as if to keep me warm. The crackle of plastic shopping bags pulled me away from the eerie scene. The Casita's door flew open allowing Mom's and Carol's presence to burst inside. Giggles and laughter filled the once-quiet interior as both Carol and Mom attempted to squeeze through the open door at the same time.

Mom stumbled off the step. and still snickering said, "You go."

With the same thought, Carol countered, "No, you..." But she bumped into her friend. Teetering off balance, their eyes grew startlingly large, their mouths gaped open, and their knees buckled. In unison, the women's rumps hit the ground with a solid thump followed by dual gasps.

Their laughter erupted until finally holding their bellies and wiping their watering eyes they recovered from their hilarity. Untangling themselves they rose and fruitlessly slapped at their soiled jeans and gathered up the spilled contents from their shopping bags.

Following Carol inside Mom plopped the spoils of her shopping spree onto the counter and turned. Her eyes swept the interior until they stopped and rested on my sleeping form. Mom smiled. "He slept through all our commotion..." But then the gaiety drained from her face. She stepped over to the couch and bent down. Like a toxic gas, a heaviness poisoned the fun-filled atmosphere and curled Mom's shoulders inward. The tight space of the Casita grew even smaller.

Carol paused in her business of rattling sacks and stowing things into cupboards. Sensing the change of mood, she turned.

Mom's eyes, now dark with dread, locked on her friend's questioning stare. Wrinkles of worry spidered across Carol's forehead. With a reluctant hesitancy, Carol asked, "What?" and then snuck a peek over Mom's shoulder at my lifeless body. Tentatively, Mom followed her line of sight. Their backs stiffened. Clenching her fists, Mom waited for her friend to say something. Carol swallowed hard. "I'm sure he's just sleeping," she said.

Like a predator the world paused. Mercifully, it allowed the women one last moment before it bared its teeth, pounced, and exposed them to the unthinkable reality that had taken over the little Casita.

Mom knelt beside my still form. Like a feather, her finger brushed across my fur. She knew I was gone. Bending down she kissed me. Her eyes swelled with tears she refused to let go. "I'm not going to cry."

Carol's voice cracked as she tried to stay strong for her friend. "It's okay if you do."

Mom stepped away from the sofa. Turning, she hugged Carol. "Why should I cry? He's no longer struggling. These last months, he's needed me more than I needed him." She pulled back from her friend and shook her head. "That's no life for a cat. He's free now to move on to his next life if that's what cats do."

She was right. I felt so light without my cumbersome worn-out body I felt I could fly. I leaned into her leg to give her an affectionate gesture, but I tripped. To my surprise, I stumbled through *her leg!* Wow! It's going to take some getting used to, living without a body.

Petunia twitched her tail and gave me a laughing chirp. She could see me!

CHAPTER THIRTY-NINE

Mom carried me back to the house. She wrapped my body in my soft pink blanket decorated with the playing kittens and tucked me into my carrier. She smiled down and gave me one last kiss as she zipped the carrier closed. "So, you will be safe and warm as you travel to your next life."

In the morning, I perched on the roof of our house because, without my cumbersome body, I could go anywhere. The sun rose over the horizon backlighting the trees on the ridge. As it rose higher its golden rays reached down from the marbled clouds and streamed across the land.

I found Mom dressed in her rain gear in the secluded alcove above the waterfall. She knelt over the smoothed fresh dirt now that covered my body which had served me so well. After gently placing the final river rock atop the others she rocked back on her heels. Sunshine thrust through the thick vegetation, crept across the alcove, and showered the scene in a golden hue.

Was she crying, or it was the raindrops wetting her face? Standing, she leaned against her shovel. Satisfied, she had picked the perfect place to lay my body to rest, she flexed her tense shoulder muscles, and a peacefulness spread across her face that I had not seen for quite a while.

"There's the bedroom window." She pointed. "From here you can see me sleeping. And you will know I'm right here…" Her voice choked. "If you get scared." She cleared her throat and raised her eyes to the sky. And if you look over there… "She pointed over the rooftop. "You can see for eternity." She chuckled and tilted her head. She added, "Of course, now you are *in* eternity." Pulling back her shoulders, she breathed in deeply and closed her eyes letting the rain bathe her face. Then with a genuine smile she said, "And it makes me feel better knowing you're so close." Blinking, she swiped away the wetness on her face and trod back to the house.

After she left, I hung back listening to the raindrops slide from leaves and land softly, soaking into the rich soil. It was not a sunny day but a perfect one for goodbyes.

And then sure enough, true to her routine. Wild Girl appeared. She plodded up the last wooden step to the alcove's entrance and made her way toward the freshly turned soil now piled with stones. If she knew I was watching she didn't acknowledge me.

An occasional whoosh of a car traveling the river road added to the quiet rhythm of the rain. I wondered what Wild Girl had seen in me. Her loyalty to me is so obvious even now. And then she glanced at me. She had known I was there. I floated down beside her. She has been such a good friend even at times I was not. We remained there, sharing a moment of understanding until a movement at the alcove's entrance drew our attention.

It was Dad! He sauntered over to us like a young Tom and sat across from us. Was he here to take me home?

"Not yet, son."

What? He read my thoughts.

"Yes, I can. Just like you can hear mine." His loud purring came across like a lighthearted chortle. His bouncy mood reassured me I didn't know I needed it.

I sat a little straighter, knowing the anger that I had harbored for him over the years now lay buried in the grave between us. And I *could* hear his thoughts. Everything in this new dimension was all so clear.

Dad's eyes darted back and forth between Wild Girl and me. "Your Mom still needs you and I want the two of you to know I'm here in case you need help figuring out how you can help her."

Wild Girl and I looked at each other blankly.

"Don't worry." He switched his hook tail and stood to go. At the alcove's opening, he had faded to only a shadow when he called back over his shoulder. "Don't worry. Everything's going to work out."

I hoped he was right.

✻ ✻ ✻ ✻ ✻ ✻

Living in another dimension had its advantages. I could go anywhere I wanted. I swooped into the Casita and checked on Petunia and her mom. Carol was busy stowing away her things for a travel day. I came up beside Petunia. "Are you guys leaving?" Petunia turned those big golden eyes on me. "My mom has to go back and take care of the last details on the sale of the house."

"Will you be coming back this way?" A melancholy wafted over me. I was going to miss those big eyes and the beauty smudge that gave her such a whimsical look.

"Maybe. Now that Mom's free of the responsibilities of her dad she wants to do some traveling."

Surprised by my lightened mood I realized I was excited for Petunia. The new adventures she would be experiencing with her Mom would be a chance most cats never have.

A tap-tap on the door caused us all to look. My mom pulled it open and with an almost too cheery expression which quickly faded to a more subdued one, she asked, "Are you packed and ready to head out?"

Carol rushed to Mom wrapping her in a big hug. "How are you this morning?"

"I'm okay." Mom avoided her friend's eyes by glancing out the window. It's done. I got up early and buried him."

Carol raised her brow. "I would have helped. You know that don't you?"

Mom studied her friend's compassionate expression. "Yes, I know. But it was between him and me. But I'm okay, considering." Despite her dead-set resolve a grin cracked across her face. "Last night every hour I woke up thinking I felt him in bed with me. Each time, half-awake I reached under the covers in the crook behind my bent knees and felt for him hoping yesterday was just a bad dream. "

Carol's mouth straight-lined with her own determination but her watery eyes gave her away. "Well, you'll get through it. But for now, how about a waffle? I made extra." Not waiting for an answer, she proceeded to fork a couple onto a paper plate, drop a pat of butter on them, and pop them in the microwave.

Mom exhaled and gave her friend an appreciative smile. "So, where are you headed from here?"

I drifted off into my new world. I knew it was going to be tough for Mom when Carol left. It was time to buckle down. That night, since it seemed in this new dimension, I didn't need to sleep as I wrangled with different possibilities to help Mom through her transition. Sometime in the wee hours, an idea had begun to stew. The more I thought about it, the more excited I became. It just might work. But it was going to take some time.

CHAPTER FORTY

Wild Girl's calico coat glistened in the morning sun as she lumbered down the steep path to the lower level of the property. Her teats, laden with milk brushed against the tall grass wet with dew. She approached the old oak uprooted by last year's storm. The fallen tree lay hidden under a canopy of encroaching blackberry bushes. There, nestled in its root system Wild Girl had chosen to make her den for her new family soon to be arriving.

She paid no mind to the doe and her twin fawns grazing in the meadow where she and I had spent last summer basking in the meadow's afternoon sun.

I hung back knowing she needed her rest. All night I had wrangled my idea around and around trying to figure out if there was a better way. But I couldn't come up with an arrangement more suitable. It was a good plan, but only if she agreed. And I knew what I had to ask of her was more than anyone had a right to ask of a mother.

When Carol left, of course, Petunia had gone with her. Deep down I had always known that's the way it would play out. Petunia was as dedicated to her mom as I was to mine.

I wished I had thought to set a plan in place before I left Mom's physical world that would help with her transition. But it all happened so fast. So now, until I can fix it, I was hell-bent on letting her know I am still here for her.

A large box sat inconspicuously in the corner of the sunroom. Mom had gathered up all my catnip toys, my feathery things, along with my clothes, which proudly displayed the Harley Logo—my denim jacket, my skull cap, and t-shirts that bragged "Bad to the Bone" and, "Live to Ride and Ride to Live." She had piled everything of mine in the box. My camouflage harness and Harley retractable leash lay on top of the heap. Resting atop everything, my Harley mouse wearing his own tiny Harley jacket peered over the rim at me and asked, *what's going on?*

I'm sure Mom thought not seeing my things would be easier, but I knew avoiding my things would not relieve her sadness or aid in her transition. What she needed was an outlet for all the love in her heart which now had nowhere to go. I was working on that but until then...

Mom never liked clutter. Everything has its place. Another justification I suppose for gathering up any reminders of her loss. But since I arrived in her life, she exempted my toys and tolerated them lying all over the house, and even stepping on them. She offered no excuses for them when visitors came. When she stepped on one, she grimaced but her mouth crooked only for a second before it melted into an endearing smile.

After rooting through the trinkets of my life I settled on my steadfast friend, my Harley Davidson mouse. Mom knew how much I loved him. His beaded eyes lit up when I singled him out from the others. Since I couldn't physically move anything without my physical body, I discovered if I concentrated on something long enough and hard enough, I could make it happen I focused intensely on him. The mouse jerked then floated into the living room and when I released my hold he dropped on the carpet right smack dab in the middle of the room. A swell of accomplishment rushed through me as I crouched behind the couch and waited.

And waited. The clack-clack-clacking of Mom's computer paused. Okay, here she comes. But then, the clack-clack-clack again. Frustrated, I abandoned my hiding place and moved over to the bookcase. Now I focused on a book on the bookshelf and willed it to move. And sure enough, it too wobbled and separated itself from the others. Teetering, it fell but lay perfectly balanced. Half on the shelf and the other half sticking out in midair. I concentrated even harder, and it nudged a little more. Finally, unable to maintain its grasp, the book dove to the floor, landing with a loud thud.

The clack-clacking of Mom's computer fell silent. The soft padding of Mom's stocking footfall grew more distinct as she peered from the hall into the living room. Her brow furrowed. *I'm alone in the house. Aren't I?*

Inside, a tide of emotions pushed against her stoic expression, yet she held her firm lips tightly sealed. Her tired eyes peered over her mental barricade and scanned the room. Finding the fallen book on the floor, she shrugged as if not caring if the cause was because of an intruder. She traipsed across the room.

Like a homing device, her stockinged foot landed on my Harley mouse squashing its catnip insides. My favorite toy squealed. I couldn't help feeling bad for my loyal toy.

Dancing a one-legged hop, Mom jumped aside. Catching her balance, her eyes recognized the offending toy. The mental barricade she had built to defend her from her recent fortress of feelings crumbled. She sank to her knees. Picking up my brave little mouse, she cradled it in her palms. As if the toy were real and she had killed it, sadness consumed her. I started to regret my ploy.

But then confusion rushed in and wrinkled her brow. Her eyes flew to the box full of my treasures that she had so carefully packed. And then just as quickly, her eyes darted back to the Harley mouse she clutched.

A battle of emotions marched one by one across her face until finally, her face melted with an endearing understanding. I thought she was going to cry. But instead, she brightened with a quiet victory. A knowing grin spread across her face, loosening the tension in her shoulders. She lifted her attention to the ceiling and then swept the room. "Okay, little Buddy. I know you're here. I know it was you." Sitting up straighter she pressed the toy to her cheek and whispered. "Thank you."

I howled with joy. But she couldn't hear. I jumped up and down. But she couldn't see me. I was only energy, a spirit but she knew it was me. I'd connected with her! If only for a moment, I was glowing.

She turned to where I had taken my perch on the logs piled beside the wood stove. She stared in my direction as if she could see me. And then she lip-synced the words, "I love you, too."

CHAPTER FORTY-ONE

Every day since we moved into this house Wild Girl arrived on the back patio at dawn and waited faithfully for Mom to feed her a bowl of kibble. But the last two mornings Wild Girl had not made an appearance. Worrying, Mom looked skyward and addressed me as if I lived in some lofty cloud. "So, Sportster, has *she* abandoned me, too?" Since her incident with my Harley mouse – which I now regret – that convinced her I was still around, she had taken up talking to me.

Of course, not. I answered back. So, who's losing it now? I was answering her even though I knew she couldn't hear me. Maybe her hunting had been successful and she's not hungry. Although that never interrupted her routine before. I decided to check in on her.

The adult tom I called Tux meowed incessantly at the entrance to Wild Girl's den. A small bird, its claw feet pointing skyward lay at his feet. I caught the slightest movement as Wild Girl poked her head out, snatched the bird, and quickly retreated inside. I was glad he was watching out for her.

My mood brightened when Tux's meows ceased and were replaced by barely audible peeps coming from the den. An awe swelled inside me. She'd had her kittens! I floated closer and entered. I couldn't be more excited than if I were the father. Sensing my presence, Wild Girl hissed, but I gave her a chirp, reassuring her I meant no harm to her or her kittens. She crouched in the corner, away from her newborns as she devoured Tux's gift. In their mother's absence, the little ones' incessant cries intensified. Five pink bundles no bigger than the wren their mother reminded me of roly-poly bugs demanded to be fed. Their pink paws seemed to wave from their pudgy bodies. Their ears lay flat against their tiny heads and their eyes were only slits. Reminding me of baby mice, my awe escaped me.

Finished with her meal, Wild Girl took no time to wash her face but instead hurried back to her nest of kittens. Lying down she nudged and licked, pushed, and pulled until she had them lined up at her teats. Their muffled peeps turned to diminutive grunts and insignificant growls as they latched on.

Wild Girl, thoroughly engrossed with her litter didn't look up. I made my leave. I would be just a distraction if I stayed. This was not the time to tell her about my plan. I would wait.

*   *   *   *   *   *

By the end of the week, Wild Girl returned to her regular schedule demanding her breakfast bowl of kibble. Mom's relief was apparent. She squatted next to Wild Girl and talked to her while now mamma cat, eating for five, crunched away on her breakfast. Wild Girl tolerated Mom's presence, even allowing her to scratch her back as Mom prattled on about nonsensical things like she used to do with me. "You know I might just let you come inside if you let me pick you up?" Mom moved her hand slowly under Wild Girl's belly in an attempt to pick her up. And just like that, the cat bolted off the patio, dove through the dense shrubbery, and disappeared.

Mom plopped back in her chair. "Well, I guess she's not the cat for me."

Smiling I added my two cents, *Wild Girl probably knows all the rules you would impose on her.*

As if reading my mind Mom added, "Did you tell her about all the rules she'd have to follow?" Mom chuckled as her eyes followed Wild Girl's hurrying along the path toward the alcove. "I know you can hear me, Sportster." She sighed as she stood to go back into the house. "Maybe I'm okay on my own. Maybe I don't need another cat."

Even *I* knew that was not true. Who's she trying to convince? She's talking to a dead cat! No, she wasn't okay.

"No one can replace you, Sportster."

I puffed up and purred loudly pleased she thought so.

But if she got a cat different from me it might be easier on her One who doesn't remind her of me. Yes, that's it! Maybe it could even be a challenge. She likes challenges. She had it easy with me. I had been quite amicable. I paced around in a circle charged by the possibilities a new cat could offer her. He could be my alter ego! Yes, it should be a 'he,' a Tom. God, I hope she doesn't name him Tom. No, she'll pick a cool name like she did for me. My mind was racing.

After a couple of weeks, Wild Girl brought her kittens outside for their first adventure. One by one she brought them out. Three girls and two boys. They hung obediently and docilely from her mouth as she deposited each in the trampled grassy area. Three carried Wild Girl's similar gray stripes. But each also had its own uniqueness to distinguish it from its other littermates. One would have thought they had spilled a can of white paint in the womb and danced in its puddle. One girl had white socks on all four feet, another a fluffy white chest and girl number three and boy four both had one front leg painted entirely white as if they had stepped into the paint can before it tipped over. As their mother plopped each one down, she ordered them to remain close to the den's entrance.

Wild Girl disappeared into the den to retrieve the last kitten. After a long pause, she emerged with the final boy kitten. Clamped securely on the loose skin at the nape of his neck, he dangled wildly from her teeth. He squirmed, jerking and swinging as his short legs flailed in the air. She dropped him not so gently into the mix of his littermates and with a twitch of her tail took her sentry post at the edge of the clearing.

Number five's eyes were not narrow slits like the others. His eyes were bigger and rounder and full of eagerness. His coat, blacker than the night, made me think he could solve all the mysteries of the universe. It gave off a black sheen that glistened like a promise. Stretching his neck, he peered over the bodies of his siblings who were still huddled together unsure of their new surroundings. He blinked in the sunshine and scanned his new outside world. Hungry for an adventure, he pushed past his littermates with a newborn's awkwardness and a big cat's bravery and set out to do just that.

Yes, he would be my choice for Mom. He was different in every way from his siblings. He was nothing like me. This guy was daring and no doubt fearless, too, characteristics that if not shaped and tempered could be disastrous. He will be a challenge for Mom. And me, too.

My candidate for Mom blinked again. Did I hear a tiny growl directed at his mother? Already out of patience with this one who had wandered too far from the fold, Wild Girl snatched him up and dropped him roughly back with his more docile siblings.

CHAPTER FORTY-TWO

It has been five weeks since I left the physical world. Wild Girl's bunch had grown from nearly hairless, mouse-like bundles into bouncing, fluffy balls of furs. Although cuddly too, the black male stood out from his siblings. His wild yellow eyes lit up like a beacon perpetually searching for some distant curiosity. His spirit reminded me of my father, and I was drawn to the promise of who he could become. Like a deceiving swell in the ocean, the little guy was hell-bent to tackle anyone who might stand in the way of his next adventure. He was a sneaker wave in the making.

Wild Girl had laid out a no-cross line for her kittens. It encircled the surrounding proximity of the den. Unlike his siblings, the little Sneaker's excitement drove him to forget the boundaries his mother had set. With energetic leaps and bounds, he crossed the line into the forbidden danger zone.

Thus, Wild Girl spent much of her time toting the daring swell of a kitten back into the perimeter's safety. Hissing and scolding him his diligent mother plopped him down within the safe perimeter. Each time with less patience than the last. I worried about Wild Girl.

I also worried about my mom. Every morning when I lived in the physical world, I waited for Mom to open her eyes. When she did, I took on the task of reminding her of the mysteries and glories the day promised.

Now Mom lingered in bed. Not in a luxurious manner and not because she hardly slept anymore. She lay there with a reluctance to face another day. She had not cried since I left the physical world. Not once. She still offered up a gratuitous smile every time I planted my Harley mouse in her path, but it was a forced and dismal gesture. As each week ran into the next, she became more and more lethargic.

I accompanied her on her errands to town. At times, her route took her past the Peoples Humane Army. Each time like a magnet, the cacophony of desperate barking and pathetic meows dragged her attention from the road. The car slowed, her breathing increased, and I held my breath. When I thought she might make the turn into the drive, I hollered *NO!* I knew she couldn't hear me, yet she stomped on the gas and sped on past the building. After her breathing slowed, she said, "If I'm meant to have another cat, the Universe will give me one."

At this point, my spirit brightened until the next time her errands took her past the facility. Each time she drove a little slower than the last. She looked a little longer, and her resolve became a little weaker. If I wanted that little swell of a cat to save my Mom from her sorrow, I needed to talk to Wild Girl.

⁂ ⁂ ⁂

I hovered at the den's entrance. Selling Wild Girl on my plan was not going to be easy. But to my advantage, I had seen Wild Girl's patience wearing thin with the little guy. But still, how can a mother imagine life without even one of her charges?

When I entered Wild Girl sensed my presence. Opening her eyes, she took a quick count of her sleeping charges. I directed her attention to the black kitten who lay curled up, deep in the sweet innocence of slumber with the rest of his litter. Only the tip of his tail twitched proving even in his dreams he was chasing his curiosity.

"I need to ask you something." I hung my head. "Even though I have no right." I prayed she would not think less of me.

Her questioning looks and encouraging purr, so trusting, spurred me on yet made me feel dirty. But I couldn't back down now. "I've been worried about my mom, you know, since I've been gone." I paused only a moment and pushed on. "She's not sleeping. And she is so sad." With my head still bowed I rolled my eyes up at her.

Her purring ceased. Sensing the heaviness of my mood she stiffened.

I glanced at the little black one and then back at her suspicious gaze. 'I know he's a lot to handle." I paused again. *Get it over with. It must be done.* I pressed forward. "I would like you to consider sending the little guy to live with my mom. She needs someone to love." My spirit sputtered, nearly dying from the effort I had exerted.

Still, she remained like a cold statue. Not even her tail moved. The quiet grew between us. And then she threw a fiery stare at me that could melt the hinges of hell.

I stood my ground. Hot air blasted around us, but I pushed on. "I've had a good life with her. She's been a good Mom. She's nursed me back from death's bed a couple of times. Because of her, I've lived a long and satisfying life. The little guy wouldn't have the freedom you can offer him, but she can guarantee him a safe and loving home… if you let him go." There. I'd stated my case.

Wild Girl's energy pinged like stinging bees. In contrast to the electrical intensity of the atmosphere, my spirit waned dangerously low.

She shifted, huddling closer to her babies who now stirred awake as the result of the crackling energy that could have made a guy's hair stand on end.

Wild Girl spat at me. Her eyes were fiery red. With a heavy heart, I turned to leave. In my wake, she hissed. Claws extended she swatted the air in my wake. She made her answer clear. I was way out of line.

CHAPTER FORTY-THREE

I returned to the alcove yearning to leave this physical world with all its hurt and pain. But my love for Mom, Wild Girl, and now, even the black swell of a kitten kept me here. I envisioned the up-and-coming Sneaker accomplishing great things. Relishing the quiet I hovered over the memorial where Mom had buried my body.

On the back patio the Blue Jay, whom I had grown to call a friend, helped himself to the kibble Wild Girl had left in her dish. I always thought she saved it for later but now I realized she left the morsels for the Jay. In Wild Girl's world, everyone watched out for one another.

A draft lifted a patch of dried leaves. They danced in a circle, and I imagined them giggling. Vibrant greenery still clinging to the branches waved and clapped. I will miss the magic of this physical place and all its mystery.

Blue Jay's shrieks of danger cut through my reverie. Alarmed, I shot up over the house and scanned the area. I spotted my blue Jay friend hopping anxiously in the fir tree that shaded the pond. Once he caught my eye, he took flight, cawing incessantly as he descended the hill and flew toward Wild Girl's den. Taking his perch on the tangled root system of the fallen tree.

Hopping frantically, he continued to call out even more anxiously than before. He drew Wild's Girl's attention at the edge of the clearing where she had been hunting. Her head popped up from the blackberry brambles. She balanced on her haunches, scanned the area, and then dashed back to her den Just as fast, she reappeared. Distraught, she belted out a series of sharp, furious mews in a rapid tempo. No doubt The little guy had pulled off another caper.

The pulse of the Jay's frenzied caws reached a crescendo. He took flight toward the river road. I shot after him.

I found the Sneaker kitten having a gay old time on the hidden path leading to the river road. He pounced on every bug crossing his path while intermittently springing over the fallen branches and small bushes while he swatted at dragonflies darting here and there. The actions of a true hunter in training.

But the seriousness of the situation did not elude me. Only a few more leaps and bounds would put the little guy in danger of the road, its traffic, and the river beyond. Of course, from a kitten's perspective what lay ahead was only another world of wonderment lying in wait.

Like the Jay I, too, flitted frantically back and forth. My anxiety increased when from the river road I heard the whine of the wheels of a truck growing louder. The kitten and truck were destined to meet. Unsure as to what to do, I knew couldn't chance using my clumsy levitation efforts. Panicked I sent a chirp to the cat gods as I zeroed in on the vehicle.

Like the Sneaker kitten, the driver was young himself. As the thought occurred to me that he shouldn't be rounding the curve at such a speed, the kid laid on the horn and stomped on his brakes. The blaring echoed up the river like seventy-six trombones as the truck skidded to a stop. Swiping at his forehead and motioned to the subject of his abrupt halt. A doe and her fawn stood startled at the side of the road. As if reading the kid's signal, the doe nudged her fawn and bounded across the road as gracefully as a ballet dancer. The fawn with its stilted gait followed and they disappeared into the thick brush. Glancing in his rearview mirror the young man revved his souped-up engine several times and then, laying rubber he squealed past the near-invisible trail opening where the little guy cowered.

Moments later Wild Girl appeared at her charge's side, nudging, sniffing, and chirping. When assured he was unharmed, she stepped back and hissed and growled with a mother's vengeance. Then with soft paws, she gave him a one-two swatting across his nose.

His eyes grew large in surprise. I wondered if he got her message. My answer came only a second later. Recovered from his bewilderment, he bounced away and then just as quickly pounced forward. Wrapping his paws around his mother's neck he tried to engage her in playful wrestling. His mom's eyes turned to angry slits. Bellowing like a lion, she swatted him one-two, one-two, repeatedly. She had lost. Blood droplets beaded on his nose from her claws. And yet undaunted and thrilled his mother had become such a challenge the little guy only wrestled harder.

Wild Girl threw her body weight on top of him and took him down. Pinning him she locked eyes with him and emitted a low growl that warned him she would take it to the next level if he moved.

Watching him I couldn't believe it. I saw the spunk in his eyes. He was thinking it over. I sensed his inner battle to take his mother on. But then he relaxed, turned away from her stare, and gave in. He may be daring but he was smart too.

CHAPTER FORTY-FOUR

I slipped away and returned to my memorial place. I needed to figure out what to do next. Wild Girl had been very clear about keeping her kitten under her wing. But surely, she understood my concerns for him. But a mother's love is strong.

I needed to rethink my strong prejudices against the People's Humane Army. Even though I was not a rescue from the Army, I could have been. On my Mom's next trip to town maybe I should encourage her to visit the People's Army. During my travels, I met a lot of *rescues* from the Army. Most were happy and healthy. And pampered.

My thoughts turned to Petunia. Some of the rescues had developed neurotic insecurities. And health issues too. Petunia was not the cat I remembered. I could never live the confined life Petunia had with Carol. She didn't even want to go outside. Granted she *was* content. So what? That she's a little pudgy?

I had been lucky to end up living with my mom. She had allowed me to satisfy my curiosities and yet be safe too. If the little Sneaker came to live with Mom, she would keep him safe too.

But Wild Girl's mind was made up. I had to face it. I needed to change my attitude about the People's Army.

My energy faded at the thought of giving up on the little guy and a chill came over me like a dread I couldn't shake. Today had been too close a call. If I didn't do something he would become a statistic. If Wild Girl didn't let the little guy go… I tried to shake off a weakness that the thought brought on. I really liked the Sneaker's spunk.

❖ ❖ ❖ ❖ ❖ ❖

My Mom sat in front of her vanity dresser brushing her hair. Her gaze flitted to the bed where I once used to sit and watch her. She shrugged, trying to ignore the cloud of sadness that now lurked in the house like a sour cooking odor. With a last sideways glance into the mirror, she pushed away from the dresser and grabbed her shopping list. She was going to town. Her route would take her past The People's Humane Army on her way to the grocery store.

Show time.

Mom slowed the car several blocks before the Army. Preoccupied, she nearly ran a stop sign. Hitting the brakes, she slammed her fist against the wheel. " Shit!" She pulled over to the curb and parked. "Maybe I should just go in, you know? And just look. They might not even have any kittens" "

Oh dear, she was talking to me again.

She gripped the steering wheel so tight her knuckles turned white. "Who am I kidding? It's kitten season." Closing her eyes, she inhaled deeply. "I don't know what to do." Taking several deeper breaths, she calmed. "It doesn't hurt to look. If it turns into an inquisition about my character I'm walking out." She pulled back out into the street traffic.

Panic washed over me. Oh no! Oh no! I thought I was ready for this! But I'm not! I can't let her go in there! The People's Humane Army. I hated them!

She had steeled herself to the task at hand. I couldn't reach her. Pulling into the Army parking lot, she shut off the engine. Taking several more breaths she exited the car.

I should follow her, but I can't. I just can't go in there! *They can't hurt you. You're a ghost. You can't let her go in there alone.* My energy was sputtering like a bad connection. I hovered behind her hiding from people who couldn't see me.

She marched up to the door and yanked it open. The souls of the imprisoned dogs and cats bombarded me. I cowered behind her. I wanted to die. Oh right, I was already dead. I skulked in behind her.

The girl behind the reception desk was addressing an older man with a large dog who hung his head as if in shame.

"Can I help you sir?" The girl smiled down at the dog and her eyes lit up. "Is that you, Champ?"

Champ's ears perked. He looked up at her and wagged his tail hesitantly.

The man nodded at his dog "Yes, this is Champ. I hate to bring him back." He slumped his shoulders so much I thought he'd fall forward. "But he's just not working out." He hung his head too, but only to avoid the girl's reaction.

The girl's face fell. Her friendly energy shifted and her back stiffened as she gripped her pen and clicked it a few times. "Oh, I'm sorry. I know Champ's a challenge, but you need to give him time to get adjusted."

The man's voice whined. His mouth twisted into a grimace. "He's chewed up two pairs of my wife's shoes. He sleeps in the garage and howls and scratches all night at the door." He looked down at the dog sitting demurely beside him, "I'm sorry, Champ." The dog did not lift his head at the mention of his name. The man rolled his eyes up at the girl and took on the look of a child begging his mother for a cookie. "We're not getting any sleep. I have to work."

A fly buzzed annoyingly in the reception area. I sent out a wish that'd he'd land on the man's sorry, blue-veined nose.

The receptionist's tight-lipped grin contorted her face. Turning, she motioned to get a fellow employee's attention. "Ryan, you remember Champ. This man is returning him. Would you take him back?"

The two employees' eyes locked in an unspoken understanding. I wondered how often this happened. After a quick exchange of smirks and raised brows that went unnoticed by the old man,

Ryan came around from behind the counter. "Hey, Champ!" The dog lit up, wagging his tail so hard his rear end swung, too. Taking the rope from the man Ryan ruffled Champ's fur. The guy hadn't even bought the dog a decent leash.

"How ya doin', big boy? Let's see if we can find a treat for you. Okay, buddy?" With a lightness to his gait, Champ trotted alongside Ryan and the two disappeared down the hall.

Oh no! I can't watch this! I wanted to fly away and never come back. I swirled around in an eddy of conflicting energies as the man signed a form and walked out the door. What would happen to Champ now? He was so happy to be back even though he had even been there before. Why was he so happy?

The girl's radiance returned as she focused on Mom and smiled. It was getting harder and harder to hate this place. How could she go on with her day like that? "How can I help you, ma'am?"

After watching the scene play out with the old man, Mom scowled at his backside as he left. She marched up to the reception desk more determined than ever. I was not going to be able to stop her.

CHAPTER FORTY-FIVE

om stood straighter, the stance she when she had to do an unwanted chore. Shouldn't she be happy? Looking forward to meeting a new kitten to share her life with? Something's just not right. And yet I knew her mind was made up. She looked the Army employee in the eye and said, "I want to adopt a kitten,"

Recovering from her encounter with the old man, the Army receptionist smiled as she examined Mom hopefully. "Sure. Have you adopted with us before?"

I knew what Mom was thinking. *And the inquisition begins.* Mom stuck her chin a little higher and pulled her shoulders back. "No. I had to put my cat down. I'd him since he was a kitten."

The woman liked her answer. She slid a form toward Mom with a kind smile. "Fill this out and sign it." Leaning to the side she motioned to the customer.

Mom took no time filling out the form. She made a couple of check marks, scribbled her signature, and pushed it back to the girl.

After scanning the form, the receptionist to an employee "She wants to adopt a kitten." Turning to Mom, she added. "Ryan will you take you back to an exam room. It will be quieter there for the kittens. You can take your time getting to know them."

Oh, man! Kittens. No one can resist kittens. I sent up a desperate prayer for Wild Girl's little black spitfire. I guess he was on his own. I wanted to cry.

I followed Mom as Ryan escorted her down the hall. Once in the room Mom pulled out a chair and sat down next to the exam table. When he left and closed the door behind him, Mom's shoulders slumped.

The last of her determination melted into a puddle on the spotless tiled floor as she braced her elbows on the table and buried her face in her hands. Like waves crashing against the rocks, a series of sobs grabbed ahold of her and racked her body. She pressed her palms against her face in a futile attempt to stop the pounding grief and cried out. "I can't do this! I can't just let you go! Oh, Sportster I miss you." She bolted from her chair and reached for the doorknob just as Ryan, carrying a pet carrier full of kittens pushed open the door.

Mom stumbled backward. Blinking rapidly, she dragged her arm across her tear-soaked face. She cast her eyes downward and blurted out, "I don't know what's wrong with me! I didn't think this would be so emotional. I can't do this now." She pushed past Ryan and rushed down the hall and out the front door. The grief she had refused to acknowledge now busted open a floodgate and flushed down her cheeks.

I sped down the hall after her. Once in the parking lot, she let go of the last bit of resistance to the emotions bottled up inside. She shuffled to her car, yanked open the door, and collapsed inside. Leaning her arms on the steering wheel she allowed the grief to overtake her. Seventeen years of love cried out for a place to go.

A tapping on the car window caused her to jump. She swiped at her tears, rolled down her window, and glanced up. A young man with soft eyes and a furrowed brow peered down at her. "Are you okay, ma'am?"

Mom nodded at the stranger. Then sniveled. She raked the edge of her palm across a saturated cheek. With red eyes and a weak smile, she rolled down her window. "I'm okay. Just having a rough time right now."

The worried lines over the man's brow faded and a world of kindness lit up his expression. "I know what you're going through.' He squatted down until he was at eye level with Mom. "I had to say goodbye to my best friend too. His name was Red." His eyes watered up and his voice cracked. "I got him on my tenth birthday. He was six weeks old." He reached in and laid his hand on her shoulder and squeezed it gently. "It was the worst day of my life." Then he smiled. "I know it's hard. But I got through it. And you will too."

Mom nodded. She choked back a sob and a couple of hiccups escaped." Thank you."

Patting her shoulder, he straightened. After giving a glance toward the People's Humane Army building, he smiled down at Mom. "They're good people in there. They'll help you find another companion to fill that hole in your heart." And then he left, leaving Mom to her sorrow.

She had stopped sobbing. She gulped back an occasional hiccup and whimpered. The man's words had calmed her. Inhaling several cleansing breaths, she scanned her surroundings. "I'm sorry. Sportster. I know you're okay. We both know I need to let you go. And you need to go on with your next life." She rocked back and forth and pounded the steering wheel with her fist. "But I just can't yet." Out of breath, she gulped. After inhaling a few cleansing breaths, she calmed again. Smiling to herself she chuckled. "But today isn't the day. Let's go home."

CHAPTER FORTY-SIX

ack home in the living room, a restorative quiet had settled in the house replacing the stale odor of sadness. Mom picked up the Harley mouse I had placed on her recliner. Touching it to her cheek, still flushed from crying, she kicked off her shoes and curled up in her chair. She stared out the window deep in thought as she absently petted the mouse with one finger. I wondered what she was thinking. She had rushed out of the People's Humane Army building as if she feared they were going to lock *her* up.

I took her reaction as a sign. The cat gods were working their magic. Maybe, just maybe there was still a chance for Wild Girl's spitfire of a kitten. I resisted the urge to check in on her and only hoped Wild Girl had given more thought about her kitten's close call yesterday.

I glanced at Mom in her chair; her chin rested on her chest in sleep. She still clutched the mouse. Was my ploy to remind her that I was still near only prolonging her grief? Maybe it was time for me to let go and allow the cat gods and Mom's Creator to take over.

I took advantage of my newly discovered levitation skills while she slept. They were improving more and more every day. Slipping the toy from her hand, I sent it back into the box in the sunroom and dropped it in with the other toys. Afterward, I floated outside to my memorial place. I needed to rest and renew my energy.

❋ ❋ ❋ ❋ ❋ ❋

As I soaked up nature's energy a thought occurred to me. Perhaps Wild Girl had taken my suggestion of giving her black kitten to my mom as an insult to her mothering. Wild Girl had returned to her schedule appearing every morning for the kibble Mom left except each time she refused to acknowledge me.

I hung back, keeping my distance and praying she would see that I was not just thinking of making my Mom happy, but I was also trying to ensure that her kitten would be safe. The afternoon shadows grew long. As was his habit, Mr. Blue Jay, certain Wild Girl had already eaten her fill, flitted down, and finished off her dish of kibble.

Mom too, had returned to her daily habits. She is an author. She's written a lot of books, but my favorite was *Activate Lion Mode* in which she was the ghostwriter for my story. Funny don't you think? Now I am the ghost, and she is the writer. She had been working on my second book when my body began to fail. But because she worried and fussed over me, my care took up much of her time. So, she had placed the unfinished manuscript on a shelf where it had lain untouched for the last few months.

After the incident at the Peoples Humane Army, she had bolstered herself, determined to push through her grief. She pounded away on her laptop's keyboard for long hours at a time. I wondered how the story would reveal itself now that the plot has taken on a new direction. The whole world seemed to be holding its breath, waiting to see how the little black kitten's destiny would play out.

A week passed. I gave in to my curiosity. I began checking the progress of training her difficult kitten. I hovered at the opposite edge of the meadow's clearing where Wild Girl kept a watchful eye on her kittens as they played.

Wrapped up in the excitement of his mission to hide during his sibling's hide-and-seek games, the black kitten was a blurred ball of energy, whooshing back and forth like a dragonfly. Five times out of ten, when he scampered up to the no-cross line, he would catch the watchful eye of his mother. Remembering his mom's warning he would skid to a stop and reverse direction to remain in the meadow's circle of safety.

But the other five times? His kitten enthusiasm overcame any intentions to please his mother. Over the forbidden boundary, he skittered without even looking back.

Wild Girl, like many mothers, gave the appearance she was napping in the sunshine. But as soon as his little paws stepped out of bounds, she came alive. Like a mountain lion taking down its prey, she sailed across the grassy meadow. Growling like a big cat she slammed her full body weight against her wayward charge. The two rolled and tumbled over and over as she wrestled to curtail her kitten. Undaunted, the spitfire of a kitten wiggled and twisted in playful wrestling until finally, coming to his senses that his mom meant business, he gave in and lay still.

My heart went out to Wild Girl. Her kittens had become more active and braver. Only the sneaker was careless. Her diligence, which had been strong in the beginning, wavered. Exhausted, she often fought sleep. A couple of times I stepped in when I caught her nodding off. With my supernatural powers, I directed a branch to fall, blocking the little guy's wayward path. Spooked, he high-tailed it back to the safety and protection of his mother.

Wild Girl ignored my presence until one day after I had sent the little guy scurrying back to her. Blinking awake she realized I had kept her kitten safe while she dozed. She sent me a sheepish glance as she licked and purred over her unsettled kitten. Before my eyes, I saw her suspicions evaporate and transform into gratitude.

When she gave me one of her seductive slow blinks which always stirred up the butterflies living in my stomach, I knew she had come to terms with what I had asked of her. My spirit surged. With Wild Girl's agreement, the little sneaker would be safe with my mom. I wanted to dance and sing.

A myriad of feelings churned inside me like winter waves crashing against the rocks. Then on the tail of my exhilaration, a flush of relief surprised me. I had become quite attached to the little guy, dreading the worst. I wondered when Wild Girl would make her move. Then like the waves being sucked back out to sea my excitement and relief vanished.

The crushing thought of the little guy having to leave his mother slammed against my heart. Wild Girl understood the consequences. The Sneaker wouldn't at first, but he was young. He would adapt.

Knowing Mom would no longer be alone, that she would have a kitten to love, thrilled me. I wanted to howl at the world. Everything was going to be okay. I wanted to chase my tail and jump so high I could touch the moon.

CHAPTER FORTY-SEVEN

A full moon cast its last rays of moonlight on the horizon before it sank into the tree line across the river. It was almost six a.m. and still dark. A constant meowing from the back porch drew my attention. It was Wild Girl trying to get Mom's attention.

Stirred awake Mom stuck her arm out from under the bedcovers and I fumbled to turn off the alarm. When Wild Girl's cries didn't stop, Mom poked her head out from under the covers and squinted at the clock. The clock read five-fifty a.m. It wasn't the alarm that had awoken her, it would not be sounding off for another ten minutes. Her eyes darted to the bedroom window. Wild Girl was the source of the non-stop pleas that had drawn her from dreamland and back to the reality of her lonely life.

If the past conversation with her friend Carol came to mind about how one of her wild cats had given her, not a dead bird or mouse, but a kitten, Mom must have forgotten. Anyway, this wasn't the first time Wild Girl had demanded Mom's attention to give her a *gift.*

She threw back the covers with little concern. Yawning and

stretching she padded to the bathroom. Mom didn't hurry as she slipped into her sweats and shoes and ambled outside. Rubbing her arms in the chilly morning air she smiled at the expected sight of Wild Girl sitting primly as usual as she presented her *gift*.

Mom's easy smile screwed into a puzzled look. There was no dead creature lying at the wild cat's feet. "Do you have a present for me?" Her eyes darted at the doormat, thinking the cat might have deposited the "gift" there. But no dead bird or mouse. Her brow knotted up further. "Is something wrong? Are you ok?" After scanning the area and finding no fallen creatures, Mom stepped closer to get a better look. Maybe she was injured.

Unseen, the frightened Sneaker peeked between his mother's legs in awe of the looming giant standing before them. I thought Wild Girl might bolt but instead, she stepped aside a few paces exposing her frightened kitten.

Mom's brows raised even higher. Her mouth dropped open as she caught her breath. Her eyes widened. "What...?" The trembling black kitten sat alone while his mother hung back and continued to study Mom's reactions.

Afraid to startle Wild Girl and her kitten Mom's words tumbled out as a whisper. "Oh goodness! Is this your baby? Is he hurt?"

The little black kitten, whose attention had remained glued on the spectacle that was my Mom, now looked longingly to his mother. Mewing he scurried back the safety of his mother and huddled against her.

Wild Girl pushed him away. Again, she stepped aside. The little guy, his eyes hooded with questions and confusion peeped out another worried mew. His mother growled and twitched her tail. Blinking he hung his head and remained where she had left him.

A heavy silence hung in the air between the two mothers as they studied one another, each grappling to understand what the other wanted. A series of expressions rippled across Mom's face as her mind clouded with questions.

Wild Girl resumed her pleading, bleating meows while holding a determined gaze on Mom until at last she read the light of understanding in Mom's eyes. But just as quickly the ray of knowing dimmed and Mom's enlightenment deflated like a balloon. She grimaced as disbelief grabbed ahold and the implication of Wild's Girl's request sank in. I didn't have to guess what she was thinking. *She wants to give me her kitten.*

Still trembling, the kitten sensed the change of tide and the seriousness of what was happening. He squeaked out another whimper. Wild Girl pulled her intense scrutiny off my mom, turned, and again growled at her kitten. Poor Sneaker hung his head, not the norm for such a spitfire.

His mother switched her tail and stepped close to her kitten. She gave her charge a tender head butt, kissed him on his nose, and then let out a couple of heart-wrenching meows that tore my heart to shreds. I turned away unable to watch. When I looked back, I saw Wild Girl's tail slip into the thick vegetation and disappear.

The little one looked desperately at the shrubbery where he saw his mother had vanished. She had ordered him to stay. A moment of DeJa'Vu swept over me. He was the same age as when I had struck out on my own. I thought he might bolt after her. He was such a small kitten to make such a big decision. And I was surprised at the decision he had made. With big eyes, he turned to Mom and stared up at her. With a bravado that belied the shivers shaking his body, he whispered the tiniest of a mew.

Like a starting bell at the race track the tiny mew set my mom in fevered motion. Motherly instincts propelled her forward. Jolted from her trance, she rushed to the shivering ball of fur and dropped to her knees. Her voice choked. "Oh, it's okay. It's okay, little one." Worrying furrows shadowed her eyes. She scooped up the little black kitten and held his trembling body to her cheek. "What's happening, little guy? Did your mom up and leave you?"

A memory slammed against me like a lightning strike. That was exactly what she had said to me the first time she met me. I couldn't help feeling some kind of Deja Vu as I watched the two interact. My spirit glowed with new enthusiasm and peace. I had loved my Mom enough. And now, I was ready for my next life and its challenges

EPILOGUE

Gently Mom lifted the shivering kitten and cooed sweet nothings into his ear. Pressing him against her cheek the little Sneaker's big yellow eyes darted in the direction of the bushes where his mother had disappeared, and he tried to twist away. A tiny pleading mew asked, "Why…?"

Mom began to sing softly, "Soft kitty, warm kitty" while she poured kisses all over the frightened little Sneaker. His big eyes stared into hers as he tried to figure out what to make of this huge creature holding him. With one finger she scratched the top of Sneaker's head and behind his ears.

A warm glow of satisfaction settled over me as I watched Sneaker Wave's future unfold. His destiny was sealed. And Mom was going to have someone to love again.

Engrossed by the tender scene before me I was startled when Wild Girl came up beside me and sat down. Always the quiet one, the wild cat looked on as Mom introduced herself to her kitten. Turmoil and sadness clouded over her, and she whispered a new goodbye she knew went unheard. I nudged her. "He's going to be okay."

I didn't want Wild Girl to second-guess herself. The decision she had made had taken monumental courage and trust in my word that my mom would love the Sneaker Wave and keep him safe. And for that, I loved Wild Girl more than anything in the world. "Your little black kitten is going to do great things," I said. "You'll see. You did the right thing."

We both looked on. Sneaker was now engrossed with his new giant who was cooing and kissing him all over. He massaged his paws against Mom's chest while his nose rooted into the crook of her neck. Wild Girl's loud purring soothed me. I felt the warmth of her kind heart and her loving energy.

Mom quickly scanned the patio area, checking one last time for the little guy's mother. Then returning her attention to the kitten, she furrowed her brow. She lifted him, so they were eye to eye and kissed him on the nose. "Don't you worry. I'll take care of you. Welcome to your new home." With a conclusive sigh, she marched inside, carrying her newfound friend.

As Wild Girl and I went our separate ways, the big-eyed excitement of the little guy's footfall thumping down the hall within the safe walls of his new home mixed with Mom's laughter and reached me like a melody. My spirit soared. He had taken on the challenge of his new life. A Sneaker Wave in the making.

And now I can look forward to my new life challenge with the same enthusiasm.

ACKNOWLEDGMENTS

It takes not only a village to write a book but also a notorious past, a courageous present, a future full of hope and love—and a critique group. Thank you to the members of the River Writers Group—Pamela Applegate, Zoe West, Tona McFall, and Heather O'Connor. Your participation during the writing of ACTIVATE LOVE MODE has not only made Sportster's story heart-warming and intriguing but you have also enriched my life while doing so. I will always be grateful.

ABOUT THE AUTHOR

As a top-ranking Amazon author, Judy Howard's writing career expands across many genres –– memoir, romance thriller, travel, reality-fiction, and young adult –– but the theme is always the same, overcoming life's difficulties.

Following her two passions, traveling and writing, Judy Howard and her cat Sportster have experienced many adventures as they traveled across the country in a Winnebago.

Described as an inspiration and a firecracker, Howard has earned her titles as a motivational speaker and a writing and marketing expert.

When Judy is not traveling, she resides in southern Oregon in the coastal town of Brookings with Sportster's "Grieving Gift," Sneaker Wave.

Website: www.JudyHowardPublishing.com
Email: jhoward1935@gmail.com
Blog: The Cat's Perspective Of Reading, Writing And Life

facebook.com/judy.howard.716